The Impostor

A PLAY FOR DEMAGOGUES

The Impostor

A PLAY FOR DEMAGOGUES

by

Rodolfo Usigli

Translated from the Spanish

by Ramón Layera

In collaboration with Don Rosenberg

LATIN AMERICAN LITERARY REVIEW PRESS
Series: Discoveries
Pittsburgh, Pennsylvania
2005

The Latin American Literary Review Press publishes Latin American creative writing under the series title *Discoveries*, and critical works under the series title *Explorations*.

No part of this book may be reproduced by any means including information storage and retrieval or photocopying except for short excerpts quoted in critical articles, without the written permission of the publisher.

Acknowledgements
This project is supported in part by a grant from
the Commonwealth of Pennsylvania
Council on the Arts.

© Copyright 2005 by Latin American Literary Review Press
and Ramón Layera

Library of Congress Catalog-in-Publication Data

Usigli, Rodolfo, 1905-
[Gesticulador. English]
The impostor: a play for demagogues / by Rodolfo Usigli; translated from the Spanish by Ramón Layera in collaboration with Don Rosenberg.
p. cm.—(Discoveries)
ISBN 1-891270-22-2 (pbk.)
I. Layera, Ramón, 1940- II. Rosenberg, Don. III. Title. IV. Series.
PQ7297.U85G413 2005
862'.64—dc22

2005017882

TRANSLATOR'S ACKNOWLEDGMENTS

This English translation of *El gesticulador* dates back to 1996 when it received a mainstage production by the Department of Theater at Miami University under the direction of Don Rosenberg. The successful 7-night run world premiere of *The Impostor* was held in conjunction with a series of activities that accompanied the establishment of the Rodolfo Usigli Archive in the Walter Havighurst Special Collections Library at Miami University in November 1996. In addition to the staging of *The Impostor*, the dedication of the archive was marked by an international symposium on Rodolfo Usigli's work and an extended residency by Alejandro ("Sandro") Usigli, the playwright's son and literary executor. I owe special thanks to Sandro Usigli for authorizing the translation and for offering valued advice to the cast that produced the play.

I should like to acknowledge gratefully the help that I received from Judith Sessions Dean of the Libraries, Janet Stuckey, Head of Special Collections and their staff in the selection and preparation of the documentary materials that are part of this volume. My sincere appreciation goes to Andrew ("Drew") Barnes for his careful reading of the text. I am especially grateful to Charles Ganelin, Chair, Department of Spanish and Portuguese, for his friendship and unconditional support.

The publication of this translation was made possible by grants from the Department of Spanish and Portuguese, the College of Arts and Science, and the Committee on Faculty Research at Miami University. I am particularly indebted to Phelps M. (MU, '58) and Beverly G. Wood for their unfailing and generous support. Their generosity not only made possible the acquisition of the Usigli Papers and the establishment of the Usigli Archive; they also contributed generously to the publication of *The Impostor*, a play that they enjoyed when it was first produced. It is thanks to their encouragement and support that the translation is now a reality.

R.L.
Oxford, Ohio

(Left) Program for 1953 production of *El gesticulador*, translated as "The Great Gesture," at the Hedgerow Theatre, Moylan, Pa. (Rodolfo Usigli Archive, Miami University Libraries, Oxford, Ohio).

(Bottom) General Navarro and other male members of the cast in the 1957 production of *El gesticulador* by the Teatro Experimental de la Universidad de Chile, directed by Teresa Orrego in Santiago, Chile. (Rodolfo Usigli Archive, Miami University Libraries, Oxford, Ohio).

THE IMPOSTOR

A PROLOGUE

"...but be not afraid of greatness:
some are born great,
some achieve greatness
and some have greatness thrust upon 'em."

William Shakespeare, *Twelfth Night* (1)

Shakespeare's famous buffoon, Malvolio, is reading the words quoted above in a letter that has been strategically placed for him to find, a letter that will ultimately bring him down. Malvolio is a social climber of the lowest rank, an impostor who fools no one. Like the central character of Cesar Rubio in *The Impostor*, Malvolio is neither born great nor has he achieved any greatness. However, I was reminded of Malvolio's letter because Prof. Rubio does, indeed, have greatness "thrust upon him" when a Harvard historian, a Professor Bolton, arrives one evening in a coincidence that is the stuff of great drama. Both Rubio and Bolton are historians, specialists in the progress of the Mexican Revolution, a "revolution" that is already being called a charade by Rubio a generation later. Bolton is interested in the Revolution as history, emblematic of the safe distance an outsider can maintain. Rubio (and, of course the playwright) sees the Revolution as a promise unfulfilled.

The Impostor begins as a domestic melodrama. Before the North American professor's appearance, we are introduced to a very unhappy family. The Rubios have recently moved from Mexico City to Rubio's hometown in the northern reaches of Mexico. In fact, they are still in the process of unpacking. We watch and listen as Rubio attempts to pull his life and his unhappy family together. The son is a college drop-out, the daughter a plain-looking girl in love with a young man back in Mexico City who has rejected her. The wife is discontented only because her children do not stop belittling one another and, especially, her husband, whom she loves dearly. In all of this it is clear that Rubio considers himself a failure in every way. Then Bolton's arrival sets into motion the events that will change everybody's lives, including his own.

Even as we initially grapple with the over-arching question of whether or not the Cesar Rubio in this play is really the legendary revolutionary hero of the same name, we are caught up in the family's struggles for a normalcy that only anonymity can assure. The playwright's "Happy Idea," is to create a character who might, in fact, be a real historical figure, General Cesar Rubio, whose body was never found after he and his men were ambushed in 1914. Like Prof. Rubio, General Rubio was born in this same town, around the same year. Rubio's death became an inspiration for subsequent leaders of the revolt that would change the fate of Mexico. For much of the first act we wonder if Prof. Rubio could really be the General and keep conjecturing as the playwright deftly gives hints that the possibility is real.

As all commentators have noted, one of the striking features of this play is the playwright's subversion of reality. Here is a Mexican play that questions realities within the context of post-Revolutionary Mexico; a play that interrogates the very notion of the Revolution. By confronting the Revolution—an event that, itself, questions political, historical and spiritual reality in Mexico—the playwright was asking his countrymen to look inward and deal with their own hypocrisies. In asking who the central character really is, Usigli is, I believe, asking who the Mexican is. And by extension, Usigli asks any audience member in any country whether or not she or he truly knows who their leaders are.

But more importantly, Usigli forces us to re-consider why we need leaders whom we know to be false. As Rubio says to his nemesis, General Navarro:

> What is each one of us in Mexico? Look around you and all you see are impostors, impersonators, and simulators, fakes, all of them. Killers disguised as heroes, rich fat cats disguised as leaders, thieves disguised as congressmen, government officials disguised as experts, political bosses disguised as true democrats, charlatans disguised as lawyers, demagogues disguised as men of good will. Does anyone call them into account? They are all a bunch of two-faced hypocrites (Act Three, p. 101).

Usigli has been lauded for giving the Mexicans their history and identity on the stage while attempting to have his countrymen recognize their *Mexicanidad*, their "Mexican-ness." We have not been taught much about the history of Mexico or the Mexicans in the schools of the United States, and this play begins to fill that gap.

We must also recognize the fact that this play was written at a time when history meant just that: "his-story." Indeed, with a few notable exceptions in either the U.S. or Mexico, "her-story" was yet to be told in public arenas of scholarship or dramatic art. Thus the two women in this play, Elena and Julia, mother and daughter, are merely objects for the playwright to manipulate in their feminine roles as defined by the patriarchy. Julia pines over her lost boyfriend while Elena supports her husband until he decides to assume the role he sees fate having given him. Elena tries to dissuade Cesar from becoming a politician but to no avail. Although she shows signs of independence she will play the role of dutiful wife, regardless of the consequences.

I began the discussion of this play by referring to it as a domestic melodrama, not to insinuate that it is an inferior play, but, instead, to say that most contemporary dramas fall into that genre. Early 19th century melodramas were, indeed, inferior dramatic pieces, meant to entertain with spectacle, outlandish plots and clearly defined stereotypical heroes and villains. And while Usigli does give us the darkly evil Navarro and his henchmen (characters that must be played carefully, lest they become caricatures), his central character, Cesar Rubio, is not a typical hero, characterized with only good intentions and nobility. He is human—perhaps the most human of the characters in the play—for he has his doubts and his decision to assume the role of General Cesar Rubio is quite possibly based on falsehoods, and, as such, he cannot be considered the noble man one would expect a hero to be. Or can he? Is it possible for him to be an honest politician, as he intends, or will he too, fall into power's corruptive trap?

Through the course of this fascinating play, we hear about revolutionary figures as well as politicians who use the revolution to fill their personal bank accounts. Fraud is a major theme in this play. Corruption and deception rule Mexico in the 1930's, the period portrayed. And, although *The Impostor* was first performed in 1947, its message is still apt for Mexicans today as well as the residents of the United States. When I was first introduced to this play I was reminded of the summer of 1974 when El Teatro de la Esperanza was touring Mexico. The reader might recall that President Nixon was on his way out of the White House that summer, having been implicated in the Watergate scandal. The Mexicans with whom we spoke were quite amused by their northern neighbors forcing their president to resign for such malfeasance. "This would never happen in our country," the Mexicans would tell us, concluding: "because we *know* that our politicians are all crooks."

Sadly, it seems that political corruption continues, as demonstrated by the "unexplained" assassination (by a "single" assassin) of the PRI presidential candidate Luis Donaldo Colossio in 1994 in Tijuana, Mexico and the highly contested results of the 2000 and 2004 U.S. presidential elections. In other words, political corruption is not a Mexican invention. It is now the year 2005 and politicians throughout the world continue to be susceptible to the same vices as their Mexican *compadres*. Perhaps this play will serve as a reminder of the sad fact that, all that we learn from history is that we do not learn from history. One hopes that the readers and, especially, the audience members will learn something from this play about their own relationship to Truth, a grand theme, indeed.

I wish Usigli "El Maestro" was with us today. Usigli was *the* pioneer. He was a man who opened doors for the playwrights who followed, a man who questioned reality in a uniquely Mexican context, a man who wrote about history as well as miracles, a man who believed the theatre must educate as well as entertain. I believe that El Maestro would be very proud that his play is as relevant today as it was at the time of its first production; a vital and essential comment on Mexicans' collective political, cultural and national legitimacy.

Jorge Huerta, Ph.D.
Chancellor's Associates Professor of Theatre
University of California, San Diego

(1) Hardin Craig, ed., *The Complete Works of Shakespeare* (Chicago: Scott, Foresman and Co., 1961), p. 629.

Rodolfo Usigli

El
Gesticulador

Una pieza para demagogos
en
tres actos –

México –
septiembre 5 – 1938
a noviembre 4 – 1938

Title page, manuscript of *El gesticulador* (The Impostor), written in 1938, published in 1944, premiered in 1947. (Rodolfo Usigli Archive, Miami University Libraries, Oxford, Ohio).

CHARACTERS

Professor César Rubio, 50 years old
Elena, his wife, 45 years old
Miguel, their son, 22 years old
Julia, their daughter, 20 years old
Professor Oliver Bolton, an American, 30 years old
A Stranger (General Navarro)
Epigmenio Guzmán, President of the town council
Salinas, Garza, Treviño, town councilors
Licenciado Estrella, local delegate and Speaker of the Party
Emeterio Rocha, old man
León
Salas
A crowd

Time: Today

ACT ONE

(The curtain rises on the RUBIOS as they give the last touches to the arrangement of the living and dining-room of the house, where they have arrived the same day from the capital. The heat is overwhelming. Both men are in their shirtsleeves. A box full of books is still in the center of the stage. The furniture is sparse and plain: two rustic, hand-carved armchairs and a sofa fill the need for living-room furniture; these are in contrast with a cane rocking chair and a few unmatched Viennese chairs badly in need of paint. Two thirds of the stage represent the living room while the remaining third, upstage, is the dining room. The two rooms are separated by a gallery-like structure: wooden arches with uncovered pillars; except for the central arch, which functions as the passage between both sections, the other arches are closed from the floor to a height of three feet by boards that are painted in a pale blue and decorated with floral designs that time has washed out and flies have spotted. Too poor to enjoy the benefit of tiles or wood, the house has a flooring made of crudely poured cement, whose uneven surface gives the furniture what could be described as an unsettling appearance. The ceiling has exposed beams. Downstage right, in the living room, there is a front door; a bit further upstage right there is a wide window; on the left center wall there is an archway pointing to a stairway that leads to the bedrooms upstairs. Upstage, behind the arches a window can be seen on the center of the wall; upstage right, a door leads to a small kitchen, which, it can be assumed, has a door to the courtyard so typical of Northern Mexico. As can be seen, the house which is made entirely of wood, is solidly built, but badly in need of repair. Due to its geographic isolation the house was not built of the traditional stone construction; the limited means of its owners did not even allow the adobe construction so common in the less settled part of Northern Mexico. ELENA RUBIO, a short, stocky 45 year-old woman wearing a scarf tied around her head is dusting the chairs near the window on the right; she positions the chairs as she finishes. JULIA, a tall, shapely but

plain-faced young woman, also wearing a scarf tied around her head, is putting the finishing touches to the dining room.

As the curtain rises, she is seen standing on a chair hanging a poster on the wall. The shape of her body is clearly noticeable. She is not the traditional small town virgin but a curious blend of modesty and provocation, of passion and restraint. CESAR RUBIO is of dark complexion; his appearance is vaguely reminiscent of Emiliano Zapata and, in general, of the men and fashions of the 1910 Revolution, although he is dressed in non-descript unfashionable clothes. His son, MIGUEL, seems younger than he is: thin, rather small for his age looking more undernourished than of slight build. He is sitting on the box of books, wiping off his forehead.)

CESAR: Tired, Miguel?

MIGUEL: I can't stand this heat.

CESAR: It's the dry, Northern heat. I really missed it in Mexico City. You'll soon see how nice it is to live here.

JULIA (*getting down from the chair*): I doubt it.

CESAR: I know you didn't like the idea of coming here.

JULIA: Nobody likes moving to the desert when they're twenty.

CESAR: It was much worse twenty-five years ago. I was born here and I used to live here when I was your age. Now the highway is just a few feet away.

JULIA: Right... I'll be able to watch the cars go by the way cows watch the train. That'll be fun.

CESAR (*looking at her intently*): I don't particularly like the way you feel about this move. You know it was necessary.

(ELENA *comes in.*)

JULIA: And why was it necessary? I'll tell you why, father. Because you couldn't make any money in Mexico City.

MIGUEL: Money. That's all you care about.

JULIA: I care about money as much as money cares about me. It's just like love. When you love someone and the other person doesn't know you even exist.

CESAR: What do you know about love?

JULIA: A lot. I know that nobody loves me. But, who knows, in this godforsaken place, I might even become the prettiest girl in town.

ELENA (*moving closer to her*): Physical beauty is not the only thing that attracts men to us, Julia.

JULIA: No... but it's the one thing that keeps them from leaving us.

ELENA: Anyway, we're not going to spend our entire life here.

JULIA: Of course not, mother. We're going to spend our entire death here.

(CESAR *looks at her thoughtfully.*)

ELENA: It wouldn't have done you any good to stay in Mexico City. On the other hand, now that you are gone, maybe this boy will think about you.

JULIA: Yes... with relief, like a toothache that went away. I won't be hurting him any more... and the extraction didn't hurt much, either...

MIGUEL (*getting up from the box*): If we're going to start complaining, I have much better reasons than you.

CESAR: Did you also have to give up something to come with your father?

MIGUEL (*turning away and shrugging his shoulders*): Nothing, really... Just my studies.

CESAR: Are you counting the years you wasted at the University?

MIGUEL (*staring at him*): Not as many as the ones you have wasted there.

ELENA (*reproachfully*): Miguel.

CESAR: Let him speak. I wasted all those years trying to keep my family together… and to give you a career… and also, because, to some degree, I believed in the university as an ideal. It's no use trying to make you understand, because you couldn't. For you the university was nothing more than one endless strike.

MIGUEL: And for you nothing but slavery. It was professors like you that made us want to change everything.

CESAR: Of course, all we wanted to do was to teach.

ELENA: The university gave you nothing, Cesar; all you received was a miserable income that barely allowed you to feed your family

CESAR: Everybody has a complaint, even you. You think I'm nothing but a failure, don't you.

ELENA: Don't say that.

CESAR: Just look at the faces of your children. They think that I am a complete failure, that I am as good as dead. And yet there's not a man in Mexico who knows as much as I do about the Revolution. The university will realize that when they see how ignorant my successors are.

MIGUEL: And what good has it done you to know so much? You would have been better off knowing less about the Revolution, like those generals. It would have been better if you'd been a general. Then we wouldn't have come here.

JULIA: And we might have had some money.

ELENA: Miguel, we have to get these books in the back.

MIGUEL: We've finally started talking, mom, telling the truth. Don't try to stop it. We might as well get it over with. Now it's the truth that's shouting at us. And there's nothing we can do to stop it.

CESAR: We might as well get it all out in the open. I don't want to have to put up with those long, silent faces, like you all had in the train on the way up here. Upset with me because I wasn't a general or a crook so that we could be rich. I don't want to go back to those last days in Mexico City when nobody talked to each other. Let them say what they have to say, because I also have a lot to say, and I will.

ELENA: You don't have to say or explain anything to your children, Cesar. Nor should you take anything they say to heart, whatever they say. They've never had anything… they've never been able to do anything.

MIGUEL: Yes, but there's a reason. Because we never saw him accomplish anything or have anything to show for his efforts. We're just following in his footsteps.

JULIA: So, it was our fault that we had to come to this place? What have we done to deserve this?

CESAR: Yes, all you want to do is to live in the capital; you're just afraid to live and work in a small town. It really isn't your fault, that you had to go and live there; it is really the fault of all those before me who thought that the big city is the only place where you can become somebody. Even the revolutionaries claim that revolutions can only be won in Mexico City. That's why we all end up going there. But now that I've found out that it isn't true I've come back to my roots.

MIGUEL: No… what you found out is that you didn't succeed there, but others certainly have.

CESAR: Did you do any better?

MIGUEL: You didn't give me enough time.

CESAR: Time to do what? To become a student leader, a demagogue? Don't be such a fool. You need more than time to succeed.

MIGUEL: That's true. You've had more time than I had.

JULIA: In a place like this, we won't accomplish anything, even in a lifetime (*she sits down furiously*).

CESAR: So, what did you have to give up by coming here with me, Julia?

JULIA: The sight of the man I love.

ELENA: That was precisely what was wrong with you, Julia.

CESAR (*center stage, punctuating his words a little*): A university professor earning a miserable salary, one that was rarely paid on time, teaching at an institution in shambles, a place where nobody could teach or wanted to learn… a university in disarray. A son who spent six long years on strike, burning tires, yelling slogans, without ever opening a book. A daughter… (*He pauses.*)

JULIA: An unattractive daughter. (ELENA *sits next to her daughter and starts caressing her head.* JULIA *moves away, annoyed*)

CESAR: A daughter in love with a dance-hall dandy who couldn't care less about her. That's what Mexico City was for us. And just because I thought that we might be able to save ourselves by coming back to my hometown, a place where at least we have a home of our own. You'd think I'd committed a crime. I thought that I'd made you understand why I wanted to return here.

MIGUEL: That's the worst part of it. If we'd at least moved to a part of the country where you could grow something, have a farm; but no, we had to come here chasing one of those illusions of yours, pursuing some hidden motive of yours…

CESAR: Some hidden motive? You don't know what you're saying. State elections are coming up and, who knows, I might be able to secure a good position. I know every one of the candidates. Maybe

I could persuade them to create a new state university, perhaps end up as the first president.

ELENA: None of them know you, Cesar.

CESAR: I went to school with some of them.

ELENA: Have any of them done anything for you?

CESAR: You don't think that teaching about the history of the revolution all those years counts for anything, do you? All the data and the documents I have gathered. I know so much about them, they'll have to help me.

MIGUEL (*with his back to the audience*): That's the hidden motive.

CESAR (*slapping him*): What are you accusing me of? What right do you have to judge me?

MIGUEL (*turning slowly around as he speaks*): The right that only the truth can give you. I want to live truthfully because I'm sick of living by appearances. It's always been the same. When I was a boy and had no shoes I couldn't go out and play because I was the son of a university professor and what would the neighbors think. When your birthday came, Mother, and we had guests, the chairs and silverware were all borrowed; we had to protect the good name of the family of a university professor... and what we served we bought on credit; what would people have thought if there'd been nothing to eat or drink.

ELENA: You have no right, Miguel, to blame us for being poor. Your father has always done all he can; he has worked hard for you.

MIGUEL: But I'm not blaming you for being poor. All I wanted to do was to go out barefoot to play with the other kids. It's the appearances, all those lies, that's what makes me feel this way. And besides, it was silly. It was silly because it didn't fool anybody... neither the guests who sat on their own chairs and ate with their own silverware... nor the grocer who gave us the food on credit. Everybody knew about it, and if they didn't laugh at us it was because they lived the same way and did the same thing. But it was so silly!.

(He starts to cry as he slumps down into one of the armchairs.)

JULIA (*getting up*): What do you have to complain about. I've seen worse... always wearing shabby clothes and looking like I do, plain and unattractive.

ELENA (*getting up and going to her*): Sweetheart, you know that's not true!. (*Holds her head in her hands and kisses her. This time* JULIA *lets her.*)

CESAR (*after a pause*): Miguel, we've got to get these books upstairs. (MIGUEL *gets up, wiping his eyes with an almost childlike gesture, and he helps his father pick up the box of books.*) Can we get through, Elena? (ELENA *moves aside leaving room for the men to go toward the stairs. Right at that moment there is a knock at the door.*) There's someone at the door. (*Brief moment of silence while they all look in the direction of the door. Another knock.* CESAR *puts the box down on the floor and answers the door while* MIGUEL *moves away from the box.*) Who is it?

BOLTON'S VOICE (*with a slight American accent*): Is there a phone here? I've got car trouble.
(CESAR *goes to the door and opens it. Professor* OLIVER BOLTON *of Harvard University appears in the doorway. He is about thirty years old and has a pleasant, healthy look about him. He is blond and has a deep tan from many hours of sunbathing; he is wearing light summer clothes.*)

CESAR: Please, come in.

BOLTON (*entering*): I'm awfully sorry to bother you but, this is my first trip by land to your beautiful country, and my car... it's sitting on the side of the road, something wrong with it. Can I, please, use your phone?

CESAR: We don't have a phone here. I'm sorry.

BOLTON: No problem. I can fix the car. (*Smiling.*) But it's getting dark. I'll have to wait until tomorrow. Is there a place where I could spend the night around here?

CESAR: No. You won't find anything for miles.

BOLTON (*smiling, with hesitation*): Well, then... I hate to impose... but perhaps, I could spend the night here, if that's alright with you. I'll pay like in a hotel.

CESAR (*after a brief pause and exchanging a look with* ELENA): That won't be necessary, but we just moved here and we're short on furniture.

MIGUEL: He can use my bed. I'll sleep right here. (*Pointing to the sofa.*)

BOLTON (*smiling*): Oh, no... that's too much trouble. I'll sleep on the couch.

CESAR: It won't be any trouble at all. My son will let you use his bed; we'll manage.

BOLTON: Are you sure that it won't be a problem?

MIGUEL: No problem.

BOLTON: Thanks. Then, I'll go get my luggage from the car.

CESAR: Go and help him, Miguel.

BOLTON: Thanks. My name is Oliver Bolton. (*He greets him and exits.* MIGUEL *follows him.*)

ELENA: You shouldn't have invited him in, just like that. We don't even know who he is.

CESAR: No... but he would have received the wrong impression of Mexico if at the first house he knocked they had slammed the door in his face.

ELENA: It would teach him not to show up at the houses of the poor. I just couldn't do that... stay in a stranger's house.

CESAR: He seems like a good person to me.

ELENA: With Americans you never know: they all dress well, they all dress the same, they all drive a car. To me, they're like the Chinese; all alike. I'm going to put clean sheets in Miguel's bed. (*She leaves through the door at stage left.*)

(JULIA, *who had been sitting next to he window, stands up and starts walking toward the same door.* CESAR, *without looking at her, calls her in a low voice.*)

CESAR: Julia...

JULIA (*at the door, without turning*): Yes.

CESAR: Come here. (*She comes over; he sits down on the sofa.*) Sit down, I want to talk to you.

JULIA (*mechanically*): There isn't much to say, is there.

CESAR: Julia, aren't you sorry for having been so hard on your father?

JULIA: You should ask Miguel if he is sorry. All this was bound to happen sooner or later. I'm just sorry I was born.

CESAR: Julia, what a thing to say! Only the young can talk like that. You are overreacting because you hate to have to admit that yours is not such a grandiose tragedy. All because a hollow-headed young boy didn't fall in love with you. (JULIA *turns away.*) Well, let me tell you something; he didn't see you for what you are, he didn't take a good look at you.

JULIA: I don't want to talk anymore about that. (*Bitterly.*) All it took was for him to look at me. If he really hadn't seen me...

CESAR: I want you to know that I had you, all of you in mind, when I made the decision to come here.

JULIA: Thanks.

CESAR: If you think I don't know that I'm a failure... if you think that it doesn't bother me that you have to pay for my mistakes, you're wrong. I also want to give you everything. If you think that we won't leave this place for something better, you're wrong. I'm prepared to do anything to give you a better future.

JULIA (*getting up*): Thank you, father. Is that all?

CESAR (*holding her arm*): If you think that you are unattractive, you are wrong, Julia. Maybe, it shouldn't be me that tells you this... but (*lowering his voice*) you have a very attractive figure... and that's what really counts. (*He clears his throat.*)

JULIA (*freeing herself, looks at him*): Why do you say that?

CESAR (*looking her in the eye, slowly*): Because you don't know yourself; because you don't know what you have. Because I am the only man here who can tell you. Miguel doesn't really know... and that other idiot, who didn't see you for what you are. (*He looks the other way.*) You have what all of us look for in a woman and, besides, you're intelligent.

JULIA (*in a toneless voice*): Suddenly you sound like somebody else, father.

CESAR: From time to time I can still feel like a man. You'll be happy, Julia, I promise.

JULIA: I'm ashamed, father, to hold a grudge against you for bringing me into this world... but what I feel is against me, not against you. I feel so sorry that I can't make you proud of having a pretty daughter! Half of the time I feel like I am nothing but one big ugly face.... (CESAR *caresses her lightly.*) one monstrous, colossal ugly face. But I don't hate you, believe me, I don't hate you. (*She kisses him.*)

CESAR: Many a time, as I watched you grow, I thought that you could have been the daughter of an accomplished, exceptional man; but, as you can very well see, until now all the knowledge I have hasn't done me much good. I often feel that all the knowledge I have is like some kind of disease, like a cancer; I haven't been able to do anything with it... not even write a book.

JULIA: We seem to be very much alike, don't you think?

CESAR: Maybe that's what keeps us apart, Julia.

JULIA (*with an unexpected childish outburst*): But it won't keep us apart any more! I promise. In any case, I don't want to stay here for very long... will you promise me?

CESAR: I promise... but you have to promise me that you'll be patient, Julia.

JULIA: Yes. (*Smiling with a hint of bitterness.*) But... do you know why I feel so bad here, as if I had been buried in this house for a hundred years? Because it feels like a giant mirror where I can see myself all the time.

CESAR: You have to put those ideas out of your mind. I'll help you.

(ELENA *can be heard coming down the stairs.*)

ELENA'S VOICE: Cesar, do you think this gringo had dinner? (*She comes in.*) We don't have much in the house, you know.

CESAR: We'll have to offer him something. What would he think ... We'll go to town tomorrow to get some food and I'll look up Navarro. I need to see him about a job.

ELENA: Navarro?

CESAR: The general, as he calls himself. He's a crook but he's the likely candidate for state governor... the one most likely to get the nomination. He probably won't remember me; I'll have to refresh his memory... It's like being born again, Elena, to start over; but here in Mexico you have to start from scratch every day.

ELENA (*shaking her head*): Miguel was right; if this was a farm, it would be a lot better for everybody. You wouldn't have to become involved in politics.

CESAR: In Mexico everything is politics... politics is in the air, it's everywhere.

ELENA: I don't know. Still, I would have preferred that you stayed at the university…

CESAR: Don't forget, though, that I lost my job during the last shakeup.

ELENA: If you'd stayed a little longer, talked to the new president perhaps they might have reinstated you.

CESAR: For such low pay? We would have starved.

ELENA: No doubt about it.

JULIA (*shuddering*): Poverty, not for me. I think that coming here was a good idea, after all. It was a change.

ELENA: Awhile ago, you were complaining.

JULIA: At least, it was a change.

CESAR: I don't know, but I have the feeling that something is going to happen here.

ELENA: I'll go fix dinner. I hope you're right, Cesar.

CESAR: Why don't you say "for a change"?

ELENA (*holding his hand and squeezing it tenderly*): Always cutting yourself short. It's absurd. If I were younger, you'd probably convince me. (*She lets go of him.*) C'mon, Julia, give me a hand.

(*The two women head toward the dining room and, then, out to the kitchen.* CESAR *picks up a book from the box, leafs through it, shrugs his shoulders and throws the book back in the box.*)

CESAR: No place for my books, I guess. (*Waits for an answer to his own question, pointlessly.*) No place… ? (*He is heading toward the dining room. when* MIGUEL and BOLTON *come in, each carrying a suitcase.*)

BOLTON: We are back.

CESAR: Have you had anything to eat, Mr… ?

BOLTON: Bolton, Oliver Bolton. (*He puts the suitcase down; while he is still talking he takes out a business card from his wallet which he hands over to* CESAR.) I had something this afternoon while I was on the road, thank you. I hate to bother you…

CESAR (*looking at the card*): A bite won't hurt, though. I see that you teach at Harvard.

BOLTON: Oh, yes. I teach Latin American history. (*Picking up his suitcase.*) I need to get cleaned up. Will you pardon me?

MIGUEL: There's a bathroom upstairs. I'll go first and show you. (*Leads the way.*)

BOLTON: Thanks.

(*They exit together. They can be heard going up the stairs.* CESAR *studies the business card carefully holding it in his right hand, tapping it on his left hand. A very strange smile lingers for a moment on his lips. He puts the card away in his pocket; then, he pushes the box of books to a corner in the dining room. While he is doing that* ELENA *comes in from the kitchen to the dining room looking for some dishes.*)

ELENA: I thought I heard you talking to me just a moment ago?

CESAR: No.

ELENA: Why did you put the books here? They'll be in the way; there was no room for the bookcase, you know.

CESAR (*after a short pause*): I meant to ask you about that.

ELENA: I thought you might be angry.

CESAR: It's strange, Elena…

ELENA: Why?

CESAR: This American is also a history professor. He teaches Latin American history in his country.

ELENA (*smiling*): Then he must be poor.

CESAR: What's that supposed to mean?

ELENA: Nothing. You know that I'm not like you and Julia who take these things too seriously. A person is born to poverty the same way a person is born dark-haired... and, look at me: I never thought of changing my hair color.

CESAR: You just think that I'll never make any money.

ELENA: I don't think that. (*Tenderly.*) I know that, Mr. Rubio, and that's fine with me. That's why I don't want you to become involved in politics.

CESAR: I wouldn't have to do that if I were a university professor in the United States or earned what this American, who is a lot younger than I am earns. (ELENA *heads for the kitchen door without saying anything.*) Elena...

ELENA: I have to get something in the kitchen. What is it?

CESAR: I was just thinking that maybe... you know how much interest there is in the U.S. about Mexico.

ELENA: It would be a lot better if they weren't so interested.

CESAR: Listen. I was thinking that maybe this fellow could help me find something in the U. S. ... a place where I could teach the history of the Mexican Revolution. Wouldn't that be wonderful?

ELENA: Right, but first you'd have to learn English. Wake up, Cesar, and let me fix dinner.

CESAR: Why do you always have to tear everything apart?

ELENA: So that you don't get hurt. I'm always afraid that you are jumping into things. You've always been a victim of that and I've done everything to try to save you...

CESAR: But don't you see? There's no a person in the world who knows as much as I do about the subject. They would be able to appreciate it.

(ELENA *looks at him with a smile, then leaves.* CESAR *takes out* BOLTON's *business card out again, looks at it turning it in his fingers as he walks toward the living room.* MIGUEL *walks in at the same time.*)

MIGUEL (*without emotion*): Do you want the books upstairs?

CESAR (*daydreaming*): What?

MIGUEL: Those books. Do you want them upstairs?

CESAR: No... we'll do that later... I put them in the corner of the dining room. (*He sits down, takes out of his pocket a pouch of tobacco and starts rolling a cigarette carefully.*)

MIGUEL (*moving closer*): Father...

CESAR (*lighting the cigarette*): What is it?

MIGUEL: While I was talking to the American I started thinking...

CESAR (*disinterested*): His Spanish is very good, isn't? He has a good accent.

MIGUEL: I probably shouldn't have said what I said to you and, I've decided to move out.

CESAR: Where are you going?

MIGUEL: I'd like to find a job somewhere else.

CESAR: Are you sorry about what you said? (MIGUEL *does not answer.*) Is that why you're leaving?

MIGUEL: I think it would be better. You see… I've lost respect for you.

CESAR: I didn't think you'd noticed.

MIGUEL: But I can't impose my views on you… Who am I tell you what to do.

CESAR: I see.

MIGUEL: You have your freedom… let me have mine. I want to live my own life.

CESAR: How are you going to manage that?

MIGUEL (*stubborn*): After what we've said to each other… and you hitting me.

CESAR (*looking at his hand*): I hadn't done that in a long time. But that's not the only reason, is it? During the strike when we were face to face, you with your fellow students and me… with the authorities, you said worse things to me… in one of your speeches. But you still came home for dinner; it was very late and I waited up for you. You apologized to me. You never thought of leaving…

MIGUEL: That was different. I just don't want to go on living a lie.

CESAR: This lie. But there are other ones. Have you chosen yours? Before it was your lack of discipline, your student activism.

MIGUEL: But at least that moved me toward truth.

CESAR: Toward what you thought was the truth. But, look at yourself. What do you have to show for it?

MIGUEL: Nothing… I don't care. I just don't want to be part of your lie, the one you're about to embark on. I'd rather find my own. (*Suddenly in a typical outburst of youthful energy.*) Dad, will you promise me that you won't do anything? (*He throws his arm around his neck.*)

CESAR: Anything? What do you mean?

MIGUEL: What you want to start with the local politicians here. You talked about it once in Mexico City and now, again, tonight.

CESAR: I don't know what you're talking about.

MIGUEL; Yes, you do. You want to use what you know about them to help you get a good job. (*Lowering his voice.*) That's blackmail.

CESAR (*genuinely embarrassed, for a moment*): Don't talk like that.

MIGUEL (*vehemently, squeezing his father's arm*): Then tell me you won't do any of that. Tell me! I will work hard, I will help you, I'll change, I promise.

CESAR (*holding his chin like a child*): Alright, son,

MIGUEL (*warmly*): Do you swear not to do it?

CESAR: I promise you that I won't do anything dishonest.

MIGUEL: Thanks, Dad. (*Moves away as if about to leave. Swings around and quickly returns to his side.*) Forgive me for everything I said before.

(BOLTON *is heard coming down the stairs.*)

CESAR (*shaking his hand*): Go and get cleaned up before dinner.

BOLTON (*entering*): Am I interrupting anything?

CESAR: Come on in, sit down (BOLTON *comes in and sits down.*) Cigarette?

BOLTON: Ah, leaf tobacco. (*He smiles.*) No, thank you, I don't know how to roll them. (*Takes out his cigarettes.*) It's hot, isn't it? Do you smoke? (*Offering the packet to* MIGUEL.)

MIGUEL: No, thank you. Excuse me. (*Leaves, towards the left.*)

CESAR (*lighting his cigarette*): So, you teach Latin American history, Professor?

BOLTON: My passion, but I am especially interested in Mexican history. An incredible country, with so many villains and wonderful things. You have no idea how little people know about Mexico in my country, especially in the East. That's why I am here.

CESAR: To do research?

BOLTON (*glad to be able to explain and to get into his subject*): There are two extraordinary figures in contemporary Mexican history that interest me in particular. So, my university sent me to do research. And, besides that, I have a grant to write a book.

CESAR: Can you tell me what you are referring to?

BOLTON: Why, of course. (*Laughing.*) But if you have any information, I'll steal it. One of them is Ambrose Bierce, an American; he comes to Mexico, joins Pancho Villa and stays with him for awhile. In my view Bierce found out something about Villa, something bad, that's why Villa had him killed. A great loss for the United States. A very interesting man, Bierce was, a great writer, and very critical. He wrote *The Devil's Dictionary*. Well, Bierce had this romantic notion about Villa as a just man, some kind of Robin Hood; perhaps he became disillusioned with him and he told him so: Bierce was very critical. And Villa was like a god of war, and gods don't like to be criticized... and he was a man, and men don't like being criticized either... and, so, he killed him.

CESAR: But there's no certainty about that. Ambrose Bierce arrived in Mexico in November 1913, he joined Villa's forces shortly after, and he disappeared during the battle of Ojinaga. There were many casualties; the dead were buried in a hurry or left on the field to be burned later without being identified. In all probability Bierce was one of them. Or he was executed by Urbina, in 1915, when he attempted to join the constitutionalist army. But Villa had nothing to do with that.

BOLTON: My theory may be more romantic perhaps, but Bierce was not the type of man who would disappear just like that, during a battle, by accident. In my opinion, he was eliminated, deliberately. Eliminated, that's the right word. Anyhow, you seem to have a good command of the facts.

CESAR (*with a smile*): Some. I have collected materials on the foreigners who joined Villa; Santos Chocano, Ambrose Bierce, John Reed...

BOLTON: Is that possible? Why, then you may turn out to be very useful to me in my research. Perhaps you know something about the other key figure.

CESAR: Which one is it?

BOLTON: A very extraordinary man. A very young Mexican general, one of the most important leaders of the Revolution. He set it in motion in the North, was the one who persuaded Madero of the need for a revolution; he was also able to control Villa. He became a general at age 23. He also disappeared, one night... eliminated, like Bierce.

CESAR (*very calmly*): Are you referring to Cesar Rubio?

BOLTON: So, you know about him? If you could help me find documentation about him, I'd pay you well; my university would give me the resources. Because until now everybody has thought that Cesar Rubio is just a myth, a legend.

CESAR (*tipping his head back, trying to remember*): A general at twenty-three, one of the key figures in the revolution, that's very true. Few people realize that he rose up in arms precisely as a result of the famous interview of the President with that American journalist, in September of 1908. He took up arms right here, in the North and he went to Monterrey with a detachment of one hundred men. In Hidalgo, while the President and the governors celebrated independence day, a federal detachment massacred all of Rubio's men, except for two, and Rubio himself.

BOLTON (*expectantly*): Yes, yes.

CESAR: Cesar then went to Piedras Negras where he was able to persuade Francisco Madero of the need for radical change, for revolution. Madero was convinced and decided then and there to publish his book on the issue of reelection. While the whole country was occupied with the centennial activities, in 1910, Cesar Rubio started the military campaign, fighting his first battles and moving around the country. He was responsible for prompting Madero to act, for securing the commitment of some members of parliament and for triggering the events that precipitated the Revolution. He also went underground and carried out various missions with Diaz's secret police in hot pursuit.

BOLTON (*very excited*): Are you sure of all this? Do you have any proof, any document that can prove any of this?

CESAR: I have proof.

BOLTON: Why, then, this is absolutely incredible. You know more than any Mexican historian.

CESAR (*with a strange smile*): There's a reason for that. (*ELENA comes in from the kitchen and, without giving any indication that she can hear, she listens to everything that is being said as she comes and goes while she is setting the table. Showing his annoyance, CESAR turns around to see who has come in.*)

BOLTON: But what is most interesting about Rubio isn't any of that.

CESAR: Are you referring to Rubio's criticism of Madero's administration?

BOLTON: No, not really. His uprising against Huerta, like his... (*Trying to find the right word.*) his... differences with Carranza, Villa and Zapata, can be attributed to his strong personality.

CESAR: What are you referring to, then? (ELENA *leaves.*)

BOLTON: To his disappearance, his death... ...something that is so out of character, something which cannot be explained. Why would such a man just disappear leaving control to Carranza? I don't believe that he is dead, but if he is, how did he die, why did he die?

CESAR (*as if in a dream*): Yes, it was the decisive moment, wasn't it? A fateful night in November 1914...

BOLTON: Do you know something about this? Tell me. Let me have some documents. My university will pay well. (ELENA *returns*; CESAR *sees her.*)

CESAR (*waking up*): Your university... just a moment ago my wife and I were talking about universities in the United States. They are major institutions.

BOLTON: Well, except for Harvard, you know... there are a few that are quite good, but they're young, too young. But, talk to me about this Rubio business. (CESAR *turns around to look toward* ELENA *who, at this point, is facing in the opposite direction, but doing nothing that would prevent her from hearing what is being said.*) Don't hold back in what you can tell me. My university is capable of investing a good deal of money on something like this.

CESAR: One night in November 1914... it'll soon be twenty-four years ago. (*He looks again in the direction of ELENA who is still setting the table.*) Why are you so interested in this?

BOLTON: Personally, I have a lot more than just an interest or an enthusiasm for Mexico, it's a passion; but in Mexico no other person has interested me more than Cesar Rubio. (*He laughs.*) I have managed to get my entire university excited about this Mexican hero. (*ELENA leaves and comes back, right away, pretending to be busy at work.*)

CESAR (*watching ELENA as he speaks*): And why this hero, and not someone more traditional, more conventional like Villa or Madero or Zapata? What about Villa? You Americans have great admiration for him ever since he had General Pershing chasing after him all over Mexico.

BOLTON (*smiling*): But don't you understand, you, who know so much about Cesar Rubio? He is the one individual who can explain the

Mexican Revolution, who can grasp its total meaning and who, unlike the others, does not join the revolution because of political ambition or to help a region like the South or, as was the case with other leaders, to satisfy a destructive urge. He is the only revolutionary leader who is not a politician, a militarist or a blind force of nature... yet (*ELENA exits.*), he can lead the politicians, control the thieves and be a great soldier, a soldier for peace, if I can say that.

CESAR: You were saying that your university is willing to pay... How much would that be?

BOLTON (*somewhat disconcerted by the directness of the question*): I don't know. I've been given a certain amount for gathering materials, but I could inquire, if I were to see some documents.

(*JULIA comes in from the kitchen, crosses the room and heads toward the door on the left and exits. CESAR'S watches her while he is talking, until she is gone.*)

CESAR: You seem to have some reservations.

BOLTON: I'm not the one who is buying, it's Harvard.

CESAR (*showing some doubt*): You Americans buy everything.

BOLTON (*smiles*): Why not? It's to advance knowledge?

CESAR: Pre-Columbian codices, manuscripts, rare books, Mexico's archaeological treasures; you would buy Taxco, if you could carry it. So, now it's your turn to buy the truth about Cesar Rubio.

BOLTON (*in the face of such an unexpected attack*): I don't understand. Did I offend you? A moment ago you were quite receptive about this.

CESAR: I am also fascinated with the story of Cesar Rubio. But all I have is the truth about Cesar Rubio... and I couldn't give it to you for just a small amount of money... or without some preconditions

BOLTON: And I will do everything within my power to meet them.

CESAR (*disappointed*): I knew that you would try to bargain.

BOLTON: Oh, no. I'm sorry. It's just a way of saying: I will try to meet your preconditions in order to satisfy them.

CESAR: That's different. (*He relights his cigarette.*) But don't you have any idea of how much it would be?

BOLTON (*uncomfortable; this is very unexpected from a Mexican*): I don't know, I would guess five thousand dollars, maybe ten thousand...

CESAR (*standing up*): In that case, I'm afraid that you'll have to look for information somewhere else... if you can find it.

BOLTON: I apologize. (*He stands up.*) If it's a question of money, I'm sure that we can work it out. My university is very interested. As I told you, I am absolutely fascinated. Why don't you give me an amount? (*ELENA comes in from the kitchen.*)

CESAR: I guess I could. (*Looking at ELENA and lowering his voice, somewhat impatiently.*) I'd say twenty thousand.

BOLTON (*raising his eyebrows*): Oh, no. That's too much. (*Sincerely disappointed.*) I'm afraid that they will not want to pay that much.

CESAR (*motioning to ELENA to leave, as she watches him,*): Then we'll just have to leave it there, Mister... (*Looks for the American's business card in his pocket, finds it, takes a look at it.*) Mister Bolton. (*Playing with the card.*)

BOLTON: Of course, I could make an effort. In fact, I will try to...

CESAR: One night in November of 1914, Mr. Bolton... the night of November 17 to be more precise, Cesar Rubio, accompanied by one adviser and two assistants crossed a mountain pass in Nuevo Leon on his way to Monterrey and then on to the capital where he was scheduled to meet with Carranza. He had sent a scout patrol ahead keeping the bulk of his forces a few miles behind. At that time Rubio had command of the largest and best organized army;

his forces had scored numerous victories on the battlefield. He was the man of the hour. His army, however, never caught up with him although it kept pushing on with the hope of finding him. When his army joined with the scout patrol ten days later in San Luis Potosi, his staff found out that their leader had disappeared. His adviser and his two assistants, one that he regarded as his favorite, had all disappeared with him.

BOLTON: But what did happen to him?

CESAR: That's what's worth twenty thousand dollars.

BOLTON (*excited*): This is what I'm offering you: I'll come up with the amount you've been asking for by combining the money from my research grant with some of my savings, as long as the university is able to cover the balance. How do you feel about that?

CESAR: That's fine.

BOLTON: Can you provide documentation?

CESAR (*after a brief pause*): Yes...

BOLTON: Then, tell me. I'm dying to find out...

CESAR: This much I can tell you: Cesar Rubio was shot three times by one of his assistants, the one he considered his favorite. The assistant also shot Rubio's adviser, who was made blind as a result.

BOLTON: What about the other assistant? You said he had two.

CESAR (*animated*): No... only one, his favorite assistant. Before Rubio died, he managed to kill him... his name was Solis, he was a captain.

BOLTON: But you said that his army was never able to find Rubio. If they had followed his trail they would have found the bodies. But it is now official that his body was never recovered.; I don't know about the others.

CESAR: When you get to see the place, you'll understand. What happened is that Rubio, as he spoke with his assistant, lost the trail without realizing it. Or, better yet, his assistant happened to make him lose his way. They were still on their way to Monterrey but not on a straight line. The detour took them away from the mountain trail by almost half a mile

BOLTON: But who was responsible for ordering this murder?

CESAR: Nobody in particular. It was really a combination of circumstances, the revolutionary leaders were trying to eliminate each other... and they all ganged up on him...

BOLTON: What about the bodies, then?

CESAR: The bodies decomposed right where they laid, in a small hollow on the side of the mountain.

BOLTON: And the other assistant?

CESAR: He escaped, blind as he was. As soon as his physical pain allowed it he searched for the bodies... he told me the whole story

BOLTON: What kind of evidence do you have?

CESAR: I have specific information about Rubio's army: municipal records from the town they attacked, reports on their skirmishes and battles, shorthand versions of some of the interviews he had, one with Madero, the other with Carranza. Captain Solis took good shorthand.

BOLTON: No, no. I mean... what proof do you have of his death?

CESAR: Cesar Rubio's own identification papers... a telegram, stained with his blood, a telegram sent by Carranza confirming a meeting for December...

BOLTON: Nothing else?

CESAR: Solis was also carrying another telegram written in code, one I was able to decipher. In it he is offered a promotion and money, as long as something unspecified takes place. There's no signature.

BOLTON: Is that all you have? (*Suddenly suspicious.*) But why do you know so many specific details about all this?

CESAR: The blind assistant told me the whole story.

BOLTON: No, I mean all these details. You have shared with me facts about Cesar Rubio's life that are not part of the historical record. How have you managed to learn so much about him?

CESAR (*with a strange smile*): I am a history professor, like you, and I have spent many years on this subject.

BOLTON: Oh, we're colleagues! I'm glad to hear that. Without a doubt, then… But, why haven't you written a book about all this?

CESAR: I don't know… no special reason; maybe because there are already so many books or, simply, because I haven't been productive.

BOLTON: No, none of that fits. (*He slaps both of his legs and stands up.*) I'm sorry, but I don't believe you.

CESAR (*standing up*): What do you mean?

BOLTON: I don't believe it. None of it is possible.

CESAR: I don't understand.

BOLTON: Besides, it's just not logical.

CESAR: What?

BOLTON: What you are telling me. There's no logic to it: a historian who does not write down what he knows. I'm sorry, professor, but I don't believe it

CESAR: It's up to you…

BOLTON: Besides, those documents that you claim are worth twenty thousand dollars… quite a few thousand pesos, pardon my calculation… do not offer any proof of Rubio's death.

CESAR: Fine. You can go find information somewhere else, then.

BOLTON (*brilliant*): But, most of all, there's no logic to it. You know what type of man Rubio was… the absolute leader, the chosen one. Look at what you are asking me to believe. A man of his stature, shot and killed in an ambush by a trusted assistant.

CESAR: He's not the only one you can find in the revolution.

BOLTON (*skeptical*): No, no. He, who was the embodiment of the revolution, dying like that, when his presence was most needed? You talk to me about missing bodies, never seen by anyone, of documents that give no proof of his death… ?

CESAR: You're asking too much.

BOLTON: It's too big a mystery. An absurd theory, really. It just doesn't fit Rubio's character, who had a magnificent zest for life, a crowning desire to lead a revolutionary movement that was good and just. It just doesn't correspond to his destiny. I don't believe any of it. (*He sits down in one of the armchairs, ill-humored and disappointed.*)

CESAR (*after a pause*): You're right; it does not correspond to his destiny, it doesn't fit his character. (*Pause. He paces back and forth for a moment.*) Well, then. I will tell you the truth.

BOLTON (*beaming*): I knew that it couldn't be true.

CESAR: The truth is that Cesar Rubio did not die from the wounds.

BOLTON: How do you explain his disappearance, then? Was he kidnapped and held captive until Carranza consolidated his power?

CESAR (*slowly, as if retracing the steps*): Rubio was able to climb down the mountain with the help of his blind assistant.

BOLTON: But why did he disappear? He couldn't leave the country, he couldn't hide.

CESAR (d*oubtful, slowly*): The truth is… he couldn't. His wounds were not serious; but, in the absence of good medical care he was very ill for three or four months. In the meantime, Carranza, as a last resort approved agrarian legislation in 1915, in Veracruz and succeeded in capturing the leadership of the revolution. This had a serious effect on Cesar's health and...

BOLTON: Don't tell me now that he became seriously ill and died, in his bed, like... like a professor!

CESAR (*looking at him with a strange expression*): What do you want me to tell you, then?

BOLTON: The truth... if you know it, that is. A truth that corresponds to Cesar Rubio's character, to the logic of things. You know, the truth is always logical.

CESAR: Alright. (*Doubtful.*) Well. (*Short pause.*) He took a turn for the worse, but not in a physical sense when he heard that the revolution had fallen in the hands of people whose motives were not pure like his. He realized that he had been soon forgotten. In many parts of the country people had not even heard of him, when he had been the one to start it all...

BOLTON: If he had been an American leader he would have had better public relations.

CESAR: Mexican heroes are different. People were mistaking him for another Rubio or for others with similar names. The popularity of Carranza, Zapata and Villa, their military victories had all eclipsed Cesar Rubio's name. (*He stops.*)

BOLTON: That sounds more human, more possible.

CESAR: His illness had debilitated him a great deal. His disappointment delayed his recovery. When he tried to come back, a year later, it was hopeless. He had been left behind.

BOLTON (*more convinced*): Yes... yes, of course. What did he do?

CESAR: His army had disbanded, his friends had been killed during the violence of those years... many betrayed him. He decided to disappear.

BOLTON: You are not going to tell me now that he committed suicide, are you.

CESAR (*with the same strange smile*): No, since what you want is a logical truth.

BOLTON: So?

CESAR: He abandoned the revolutionary movement, completely disillusioned and without a cent to his name.

BOLTON (*anxiously*): But he's alive!

CESAR (*still smiling*): He's alive.

BOLTON: I'll pay you the amount you requested if you can show me proof.

CESAR: What kind of proof do you want?

BOLTON: The man himself. I want to see him.

(*ELENA goes from the kitchen to the dining room carrying napkins and some bread.*)

CESAR: You have to promise me that you won't tell anyone. Without you meeting that condition I wouldn't strike a deal with you; not for a million dollars.

BOLTON: Why?

CESAR: You have to promise me. He does not want anyone to know that he is alive.

BOLTON: But why?

CESAR: I don't know. Perhaps he hopes that his people may remember him one day... and wish and hope that he may come back.

BOLTON: But I can't promise you not to tell anyone. I intend to return to the United States and to teach what I know, my students expect that from me.

CESAR: You can say that he's alive; but that you can't tell anyone where he lives. (*ELENA heads towards the kitchen.*)

BOLTON (*shaking his head*): History is not like a novel. My students expect to hear the facts and to make sense of the facts; they pay for their education not for a dream, or a myth.

CESAR: And yet, history is no more than a dream. Those who made history dreamed with goals that could not be accomplished; those who study history only dream about the past; those who teach it, (*with a smile.*) only dream that they have the truth and can pass it on...

BOLTON: What do you want me to promise you, then?

CESAR: Promise me not to reveal Cesar Rubio's current identity. (*ELENA goes to the kitchen and returns with a steaming soup tureen.*)

BOLTON (*a pause*): Can I divulge the rest... and prove it?

CESAR: Yes.

BOLTON: It's a deal. (*Stretches his hand out.*) When are you going to take me to see him? Where is he?

CESAR (*with a subdued voice*): Maybe you'll get to see him sooner than you would imagine.

BOLTON: What has he been doing since he disappeared? He is not the type of person to remain idle.

CESAR: No.

BOLTON: Did he stop being a revolutionary?

CESAR: Let's just say that he chose an obscure, humble profession...

BOLTON: Him? Well, I guess. Did he become a farmer? He did believe in the importance of the land.

CESAR: Perhaps, but the climate wasn't right...

BOLTON: That's true.

CESAR: There were other responsibilities... someone had to uphold the spirit of the revolution and to raise it above the personal weaknesses of its leaders...

BOLTON: Yes, Rubio would be able to do that, but how?

CESAR (*with his voice still subdued*): There are different ways. To raise, for example the revolution to an intellectual level, to be able to explain it to others.

BOLTON: What do you mean?

CESAR: To be, on the surface, an ordinary man... like you... or like me... a professor of history of the revolution, for example.

BOLTON (*as if struck by lightning*): You?

CESAR (*after a pause*): Have I said that?

BOLTON: No... but... (*Reacting abruptly, he stands up.*) Now I understand. Now I know why you did not want to make everything public, to tell the truth! (*CESAR looks at him without saying anything.*) That explains everything, doesn't it?

CESAR (*He nods in the affirmative. Measuring his words, looking into the distance without paying attention to ELENA, who is staring intently at him from the dining room*): Yes... that would explain everything. How a man who has been forgotten, betrayed, who has seen how the revolution has turned into a big lie; how this man could decide that he wants to teach history... .the truth about the history of the revolution.

(*ELENA, dumbstruck, without gesturing, takes a few steps toward the arches.*)

BOLTON: Yes. This is absolutely incredible. But you...

CESAR (*with that strange smile of his*): But don't you find this hard to believe, almost absurd?

BOLTON: It's too powerful, too... heroic. But it does correspond to his character. Can you prove this?

ELENA (*walking into the living-room*): Dinner is ready. (*She goes to the door, left, calling out.*) Julia! Miguel! Dinner! (*MIGUEL can be heard coming rapidly down the stairs.*)

BOLTON (*to* ELENA): Thank you, ma'm. (*To* CESAR) Can you? (*CESAR nods affirmatively.* MIGUEL enters with JULIA following right behind.)

ELENA (*to* BOLTON): Please, come in.

BOLTON (*deep in thought*): Thank you. (*Heads toward the dining room. Suddenly he turns around facing CESAR, who is standing motionless.*) It's absolutely incredible!.

MIGUEL (*with a quizzical look*): Come in.

BOLTON: Incredible. Oh, thanks.

ELENA: Go on and start serving, Julia, please.

(*JULIA walks into the dining room. MIGUEL, who is still standing at the door, looks with suspicion at BOLTON, then at CESAR sensing something strange about them. CESAR, conscious of his watchful gaze, takes a few steps toward the front, right. ELENA follows him.*)

ELENA: Cesar...

CESAR (*turns around quickly, looking at MIGUEL*): Go into the dining room and keep Mister (*looks at the card.*) Bolton company. (*To BOLTON.*) Go on without me. I have to wash. (*Turns toward the left still under MIGUEL's gaze, who, after letting BOLTON go by, shrugs his shoulders and goes in.*)

ELENA (*who has followed CESAR to the left, stops him holding him by the arm*): Why did you do that, Cesar?

CESAR (*breaking free*): I have to wash.

ELENA: Why did you do it? You know it's not right. You know (*under her breath.*) you lied.

(*CESAR throws his shoulders back and exits. ELENA remains standing in the same spot and watches him leave. His steps can be heard on the stairs. Voices can be heard in the dining room.*)

JULIA: Please sit down, sir.

BOLTON: Thank you. Things like this can only happen in the Mexican Revolution, don't you think?

MIGUEL: What are you talking about?

BOLTON: Extraordinary men like...
(*Almost at the same time*):

ELENA (*reacting abruptly and heading deliberately toward the dining-room*): The children don't know anything about that, Professor. They're too young.

BOLTON (*standing up, absolutely convinced by now*): Oh, of course, Ma'am. I understand... but, it's still absolutely incredible.

CURTAIN

ACT TWO

(*Four weeks later, in Professor CESAR RUBIO'S house. It's five o'clock in the afternoon. Its is a suffocatingly hot and dry day. The door and windows are all open. JULIA tries to read a book; from time to time she puts it down and uses it like a fan. Her shapely figure can be easily discerned through the extremely thin summer dress that she is wearing. She drops the book with boredom, leans out the window, right. Suddenly she calls out.*)

JULIA: Is that the mailman? (*A moment later, she turns around looking frustrated. She picks up the book and again looks out of the window. While she is still looking out the window, THE STRANGER (NAVARRO) shows up at the door on the right and stops. He is a tall, energetic fifty two year old man. He is white-haired but his kayser-style twisted end mustache is so dark that it has the appearance of being dyed. He is dressed like a northener in very light clothes. He stands still, with his hands on his hips, studying the room. Upon seeing JULIA'S figure outlined against the window he smiles and instinctively reaches for the end of his mustache. JULIA, turns around, standing up. She is startled when she sees the strange*r.)

STRANGER: Good afternoon. Pardon me, Miss but I I'm told that Cesar Rubio lives here. Is that true?

JULIA: I'm his daughter.

STRANGER: Ah. (*He twists the end of his mustache, again.*) So he does. I see. Mmm… strange.

JULIA: Why do you say that?

STRANGER: And where is he?

JULIA: I don't know. He's out.

STRANGER (*with a gesture of annoyance*): I'll be back, I have to see him to believe it.

JULIA: You can leave your name, if you wish. I'll tell him you stopped by.

STRANGER (*after a pause*): I'd rather give him a surprise. I'm an old friend of his. Good bye, Miss. (*He twists the end of his mustache and smiles brazenly while staring at JULIA up and down from head to toe. She shudders uncomfortably. He repeats, while staring at her.*) I'm a friend. An old friend. (*Smiles to himself.*) And I hope to see you again, Miss.

JULIA: Good bye.

STRANGER (*swaggering slightly he walks toward the door; at the door he turns around to look at her*): See you next time, Miss. (*Exits.*)

(*JULIA shrugs her shoulders. ELENA'S steps can be heard on the stairs. JULIA goes back to her reading.*)

ELENA (*as she comes in*): Who was that? Was it the mailman?

JULIA: No, it was a man who says he's an old friend of father's. He said that in a very strange way. He also said that he'd come back. I didn't particularly like the way he looked at me.

ELENA (*pointedly*): Did I hear you say that the mailman did not come by?

JULIA: He did come ... but there was nothing for us.

ELENA: Were you expecting a letter?

JULIA: No.

ELENA: I don't like it when you lie to me. I know very well that you wrote a letter to that boy. Why did you do it? (*JULIA does not an-*

swer.) You know that women are not supposed to do that. All you are doing is torturing yourself, waiting and waiting, for nothing.

JULIA: I have nothing better to do in this place. Just leave me alone, Mother. (*She shudders.*)

ELENA: What's the matter?

JULIA: Oh, nothing. It's the man who came looking for father, the way he looked at me. (*Sudden transition. Throws the book down.*) Is this the way we are going to spend the rest of our lives? I just can't stand it any longer.

ELENA (*shaking her head*): That's not what's troubling you, Julia. It's the memory of Mexico City. If you could only forget that boy; it would make it a lot easier for you to accept your life here.

JULIA: I don't see any future for us here. And what is Father doing about it? He leaves in the morning, he comes back at night without ever solving anything, without ever paying any attention to us. For weeks now, it's been impossible to talk to him without his becoming annoyed at us. He seems like a different person. I wonder if he has ever cared for us.

ELENA: He's just unhappy that things are not going well for him. But, Julia, you shouldn't let those bad feelings poison your heart.

JULIA: Miguel is also feeling hopeless. And with reason.

ELENA: But you should be more patient... where is your brother now?

JULIA: He went to town to look for a job. He says he's leaving. I don't blame him. I should...

ELENA: What can we do with children like you? You are so impatient. Why can't you be more understanding? You are impatient with your father when things don't work out for him, but you are perfectly willing to wait patiently for a letter from a man who couldn't care less about you.

JULIA: That's a mean thing to say, Mother.

ELENA: What is really hurting you, Julia, is the truth. (*JULIA stands up and walks toward the left.*) We need to iron those clothes. Could you, please, bring them in? They're hanging out in the yard. (*JULIA without saying anything, walks to the dining-room and from there to the kitchen and out to the yard. ELENA watches her go by, shaking her head, and goes out to the kitchen. The stage remains empty for a moment. CESAR walks in from the right with his jacket in his arm; his shoes are dusty. He throws his jacket on a chair and lays down on the couch wiping off his forehead. While he is laying down he methodically, as is his custom, rolls a cigarette. He lights it up and smokes. ELENA enters the dining room, smells the smoke from the cigarette and immediately heads out toward the living room.*)

ELENA: Why didn't you tell me that you'd come back?

CESAR: Get me a glass of water with a lot of ice.

(*ELENA goes back to the dining room and returns with the glass of water; CESAR sits up and drinks slowly.*)

ELENA: Did you find anything?

CESAR (*handing the empty glass over*): Don't you think that I would have told you if I had. But, no, you have to keep after me, pestering me with questions and… (*stops suddenly.*)

ELENA (*turning the glass in her hands*): Julia is right… for weeks now you seem to have nothing but hatred for us, Cesar.

CESAR: For weeks now all of you, and I mean all of you, watch me like a hawk. You spy on me, watching my every move, looking for signs on my face of I don't know what…

ELENA: Cesar!

JULIA (*comes in carrying a bundle of clothes*): Here are the clothes, mother.

ELENA (*goes to the dining-room to put down the glass*): Leave them right here or, maybe not. We have to sew a couple of buttons before we iron them. Would you like to do that in your room?

(*JULIA keeps going, without giving an answer, toward the living-room, turns left without saying anything to her father.*)

CESAR (*looking at her*): Is the heat still bothering you, Julia?

JULIA (*without looking at him*): Not as much as my own problems. (*Exits.*)

CESAR; Did you hear that? I don't know what you've told them about me but I feel that my own children are turning against me.

ELENA (*slowly but firmly*): It's all in your mind, Cesar; you are just afraid to face the truth. You blame whatever is bothering you and making you feel the way you do on us, on me especially. It's not us. It's you…

CESAR: What do you mean by that?

ELENA: You know exactly what I mean.

CESAR (*dropping down to his seat*): That's it. Why don't you tell me exactly what you mean?

ELENA: I couldn't tell you what your own conscience can tell you, Cesar. You've been like this ever since Bolton left, ever since you closed the deal with him.

CESAR (*standing up, furious*): Didn't I just tell you? Spying on me. You were snooping around that night, weren't you?

ELENA: I just heard by chance and I reminded you that it is wrong to lie.

CESAR: I did not lie. Since you heard everything you must know that I didn't contradict him. I only sold him what he wanted to buy.

ELENA: You spoke with such assurance that it left no room for doubt. I don't know how you could do it, Cesar, much less understand why you should be so surprised that your lies are catching up with you.

CESAR: Well, suppose it was the truth.

ELENA: But, it wasn't.

CESAR: Why not? You met me long after that happened.

ELENA: Cesar, are you saying that only to convince yourself?

CESAR: You're wrong.

ELENA: You can fool yourself, if you want. But you won't fool me.

CESAR: You're right. Still, why couldn't it be possible? We have the same name... we were born right here in the same town; we were about the same age.

ELENA: But you did not share the same destiny. His destiny does not belong to you.

CESAR: Bolton believed everything. What I told him was precisely what he wanted to believe.

ELENA: And you are convinced that you did nothing wrong by telling that?

CESAR: And why didn't you speak up, then? Why didn't you denounce me in front of Bolton, in front of the children?

ELENA: I wanted to, but I didn't. Instead, I went along with your lie.

CESAR: Why did you do that?

ELENA: You'd have to be a woman to understand. I don't want to judge you, Cesar... but this can't go on.

CESAR: Go on? What do you mean?

ELENA: I saw the package you brought last night... the uniform, the wide-brimmed hat.

CESAR: You were spying on me, then!

ELENA: Yes, I was... I don't want you to continue to deceive yourself. You'll end up believing that you are some kind of hero. And I also want to ask you something: what are you going to do with all that money?

CESAR: I don't have to report everything to you...

ELENA: It's not so much the money I am concerned with. I've never known what to do with it anyway. What I'm really concerned with is the children... they're so desperate and confused.

CESAR: You're right. I have thought about them, about you, many times. I have tried to do something. I've been to Saltillo, to Monterrey. I looked at houses, at furniture. But, for some reason, I couldn't bring myself to buy anything. (*Lowers his head.*) Except for that uniform... which makes me think that I'm really a general.

ELENA: Aren't you worried that someone might find out?

CESAR; That won't happen. Bolton promised me. No one will find out.

ELENA: Oh, Cesar. you never change. Why don't we just leave? The children need a change... a real change. Let's move, Cesar... I know that you have enough money... I don't care how much. Now that you have some... having to hide it is what makes you behave the way you do

CESAR: I don't know if I have the right to spend it. That's what's troubling me so much. Do I have the right to spend it on the children?

ELENA: So, you do have the money. I just can't see you getting rid of that money, now that you have it; I couldn't. I am worried about the children, I'm really concerned about their future.

CESAR: Getting rid of the money? I've thought about it, but I couldn't. I am also ashamed to admit it, but I have even considered going away, alone.

ELENA: I knew it. Every night you've been late I've wondered: I've said to myself, that's it, he's not coming back.

CESAR: It wasn't because I had stopped loving you… you can be sure of that.

ELENA: I know that… It was really remorse, Cesar.

CESAR (*transition*): Why should it be remorse? Other people have done worse, they've even committed crimes, especially in Mexico City. I did not steal anything from anyone, I didn't ruin anybody's life.

ELENA: You know that if the truth comes out, Bolton for one thing, who is younger and inexperienced, would lose his reputation. His career would be ruined. Since we don't have anything, we'd end up losing our peace of mind. Why don't we go somewhere else, Cesar?

CESAR: If Bolton himself did find out anything, he'd have to keep quiet to avoid getting involved. And where would we go? Back to Mexico City?

ELENA: You'd never feel safe there.

CESAR: Monterrey? Saltillo? Tampico?

ELENA: Could you possibly feel safe anywhere in this country, Cesar? I'd always be afraid for you.

CESAR: I don't know what you mean.

ELENA: You know very well… you know that you'd always have to deal with the ghost of…

CESAR (*defiant*): You'll end up making me feel like a criminal. (*Pause.*) Why don't we go to the United States? To California?

ELENA: That might be the best thing to do, Cesar.

CESAR: I just can't see myself leaving Mexico.

ELENA: Nothing is stopping you, only those ideas and dreams of yours.

CESAR: Dreams! What you don't understand is that reality is all I care for. The kind of reality… (*Shrugs his shoulders.*) I've wanted to go to California for a long time; but it couldn't be permanently. (*Forcefully.*) You ended up scaring me; no, we are not going anywhere; we're staying right here, there's nothing to fear.

ELENA: So, you did get scared. You also felt remorse, didn't you? Don't you realize that it is all in your head?

CESAR: If anyone heard you they'd think that it was something terrible, that I committed some horrible crime. No, I have not committed any crime. What you call remorse is just confusion. If I haven't spent any of the money it's because I had never had so much at one time… in my entire life. Like most people who are poor, I've lost the ability to spend. Others lose their appetite when they do not have enough to eat.

ELENA: What you say makes a lot of sense, it seems quite logical, Cesar.

CESAR: Well, then?

ELENA: It just seems that way, because you intellectualize things. But it isn't true, Cesar. It just appears like you did not commit a crime when you took on the identity of a dead person in order to…

CESAR: That's enough!

ELENA: It may very well be that you did not do anything wrong. But why do you feel and act as if you committed a crime?

CESAR: That's not true!

ELENA: You accuse me of spying on you, of hating you… you hide from us every day… the truth is, it's you who is spying on yourself I lay awake every night thinking about it It's you who is starting to hate us… it's like when someone is going crazy, don't you see?

CESAR: What do you want me to do, then? (*Pause.*) Or are you asking for your cut?

ELENA: No, Cesar, with the kind of life we've had together I am like those people who don't have enough to eat: I've lost my appetite. I'm not complaining. But Miguel said that he was staying only because you had promised him not to do anything dishonest.

CESAR: And have I done anything like that?

ELENA: You are the one who knows better than I; but, Cesar, your children are paying a heavy price with this stagnation. We are old, we don't need the money the way they do. You could help them establish themselves somewhere else. You could give all the money to them in order to get rid of those ideas of yours. It wouldn't hurt you or me to be poor a few more years.

CESAR (*showing his frustration*): What about us? Don't we also have the right?

ELENA: That's up to you. But don't sacrifice the children. Maybe you don't want to leave Mexico because you want people to find out that we have money, out of vanity. If we go some place, Cesar, we'll be happy. We could have a little shop, start a Mexican restaurant, anything. Miguel still believes in you, in spite of everything.

CESAR: Leave me alone! Why are you forcing me to make decisions right now? There'll be time… plenty of time. (*Pause.*) You know me too well.

ELENA: Plenty of time. It'll be too late. Don't hate me, Cesar. (*Holds his hand.*) We've always protected each other. Deep down, you're honest. Why do you feel ashamed of that? Why are you trying to be something else?… now?

CESAR: Everybody here lives by appearances, through gestures. I have claimed that I am the other Cesar Rubio. Is that going to hurt anyone? Look at those who are generals but never set foot on a battlefield, or those who claim to represent the people when all they do is steal from them; demagogues who agitate the workers and call them comrades without ever holding a real job or getting their hands dirty; professors who don't know how to teach; students who never touch a book. Look at Navarro, the likely candidate for state governor... I know that he is nothing but a crook, I have proof of it, and he is regarded as a hero, a national political figure. They are the ones who hurt people and they profit from their lies. I am a lot better than most of them. Why not?

ELENA: Because you know it... that's something you carry within yourself. Not you, not you, absolutely not...

CESAR: You stupid idiot! Leave me alone! Get away from me!.

ELENA: You are blind, Cesar.

(*MIGUEL comes in, he is carrying his jacket in his arm and a folded newspaper in his hand. He seems upset. CESAR and ELENA stop talking but their voices seem as if they are still ringing in the air. CESAR paces back and forth. MIGUEL sits down on the sofa; he looks tired, as he watches both of his parents for a few seconds.*)

ELENA: Where were you, Miguel? (*MIGUEL does not answer; He continues to look at CESAR very intently. The light in the room fades and grows dimmer as if covered by dust.*)

CESAR (*turning around as if bitten by something*): Why are you looking at me like that, Miguel?

MIGUEL (*slowly*): I've just been thinking that your children know very little about you, father.

CESAR: About me? You don't know anything. You've never cared enough to want to know about me.

MIGUEL: But I also wonder if mother knows more about you than we do, or if she is hiding something from us.

ELENA: Miguel, what's the matter with you? Are you accusing me of…?

MIGUEL: Nothing is the matter with me. It's strange, though, that in order to know who my own father is I have to wait until I read about it in the newspapers.

CESAR: What are you talking about?

MIGUEL (*unfolding the newspaper*): Here. They are talking about you.

CESAR (*going towards him*): Let me see.

MIGUEL (*with contained energy, almost rhythmically*): No. I'll read it to you. At least, I learned how to do that. (*CESAR and ELENA exchange a quick glance.*)

ELENA (*in a low voice*): Cesar!

MIGUEL (*reading slowly, emphasizing the words*): "A great Mexican hero reappears. Truth is stranger than fiction. Under this title, taken from Shakespeare, Professor Oliver Bolton of Harvard University publishes in the "New York Times" a series of articles on the Mexican Revolution."

CESAR: Go on.

(*ELENA moves closer to him and holds on to his arm, which she squeezes gradually throughout MIGUEL's reading of the newspaper article.*)

MIGUEL (*after looking at his father; reads in a low tone of voice*): "The first article describes the mysterious disappearance, in 1914, of the extraordinary figure of General Cesar Rubio, as it turns out a true forerunner of the revolution. Bolton describes Rubio's sudden and precocious rise to power, the influence he had on the future of Mexico and its leaders, until he was set upon in an ambush and gunned down by one of his subordinates, someone who had been paid by his enemies. The article reproduces documents which are apparently authentic and, the result of serious scholarship."

ELENA: And he gave you his word, didn't he?

CESAR: Be quiet.

MIGUEL (he *looks at them, smiles strangely, and continues reading*): "These revelations will create quite a stir in political circles and will, no doubt, alter the official record of contemporary Mexican history. But the most dramatic revelation appears in the second article; in it Bolton reveals his most recent discovery in Mexico. It so happens, according to Bolton, that Cesar Rubio is alive. Disillusioned by the victory of the demagogues and false revolutionary leaders and relegated to virtual anonymity and oblivion, he lives, contrary to general belief, and dedicates himself as an obscure university professor (he makes a few thousand pesos a month, barely a couple of hundred dollars at the current rate of exchange) to teaching the history of the revolution in order to rescue it for future generations. (*MIGUEL raises his eyes and looks at CESAR, who turns his face away. JULIA's steps can be heard on the stairs.*) Upon shaking the hand of this hero, says Bolton, I promised to hide his current identity. But I cannot resist the beauty of truth, the desire to do justice to a man whose behavior has no parallel in history."

JULIA (*entering*): Mother.

MIGUEL (*turning towards her*): Listen. (*He reads.*) "Quite worthy of national recognition, Cesar Rubio can still serve his country well, a nation which more than ever needs disinterested, altruistic men like him. Cincinnatus withdrew from public life to toil the land and became a successful farmer. Julius Caesar wrote his *Commentaries of the Gallic Wars;* but neither these nor other heroes can compare with Cesar Rubio, the great chieftain of yesteryear, the humble professor of today. Truth is stranger than fiction" (*Pause.*)

JULIA: What is this all about… ?

MIGUEL: There is more. (*He reads.*) "Professor Bolton declared to foreign correspondents that he had found Cesar Rubio living in an isolated, modest wooden home near the town of Allende, not far from the central highway."

ELENA: Oh, Cesar.

JULIA: I don't understand, Father. Are they talking about… ?

CESAR: Is that all?

MIGUEL: No, there's more. But first tell Julia that they are talking about you, Father.

CESAR: Go on. Finish.

MIGUEL: "Under strict orders from the President the Department of Defense and the Revolutionary Party are now conducting a thorough investigation of the case. Without a doubt, this major development will radically transform the contemporary political scene in Mexico." That's it.

ELENA: What are you going to do now, Cesar?

CESAR: You were right. We have to leave right away.

MIGUEL: But I want to know. Is any of this true? And if it is true, why have you kept it a secret for so long, Father?

JULIA (*lifting her eyes from the newspaper*): You, Father… it seems so strange!

MIGUEL: Well, are you going to tell me?

ELENA: You are questioning your father, Miguel.

MIGUEL: But, don't you understand, Mother? I have every right to know.

JULIA (*throwing the newspaper, she runs and throws her arms around CESAR*): And you have made all these sacrifices all these years, Father? I didn't know. Oh, Father, you make me so happy! I feel so bad because I didn't… (*CESAR returns the embrace in such a way that he can hide the expression of shock in his face…*)

MIGUEL: Are you going to tell me?

JULIA (*freeing herself, vehemently*): And what makes you think that it isn't true? We ought to feel ashamed of the way we have treated him, (*Smiling.*), the way we have treated General Cesar Rubio.

MIGUEL: Father, are you going to tell me?

CESAR: Well…

ELENA: We must leave at once, Cesar. What we wanted to avoid is happening already. Miguel, Julia, pack up your things right away. We are going to the United States. We'll catch the 7:00 o'clock train.

CESAR (*finally persuaded*): Yes, we're leaving.

(*JULIA heads towards the left.*)

MIGUEL: But this looks like we're running away. Why? Why isn't anyone saying anything? All I want to hear is one word…

JULIA (*turning around*): Come on, Miguel, let's go.

CESAR (*making an effort*): We will explain everything later. Now we have to pack up and go.

(*MIGUEL casts one last glance at his father and heads toward the left. At the moment when he meets up with JULIA near the door, a knock can be heard coming from the right. CESAR and ELENA give each other a look of helplessness.*)

CESAR (*in a weak voice*): Who is it?

(*Five men come in from the right in the following order: Epigmenio GUZMAN, the mayor of the town of Allende, next, Señor ESTRELLA, attorney, delegate of the Revolutionary Party and gifted orator; following them, SALINAS, GARZA and TREVIÑO, state representatives. Instinctively, ELENA holds on to CESAR's arm forcing him to take a couple of steps back. JULIA stands behind CESAR on the other side with MIGUEL next to his mother. The family group is disconcerting to the newcomers.*)

GUZMAN (*clearing his throat*): Are you the man who claims to be General Cesar Rubio?

CESAR (*after casting a quick glance at his family, he steps forward*): That's my name.

SALINAS (*taking a step forward*): But are you the General?

GUZMAN: Allow me, colleague Salinas, Let me handle this.

ESTRELLA: Pardon me, gentlemen, but I believe I am the person who should deal with this matter. (*Pulling out a telegram.*) Besides, I have special instructions.

(*ESTRELLA is a tallish, thin man whose coarse features are evidence of racial mixture. He wears long sideburns and many rings on his fingers. His complexion show clear signs of both excess and deprivation in matters of the flesh. The other men are typical northerners. SALINAS and TREVIÑO are thin while GARZA and GUZMAN are heavy. They are all wholesome-looking, beer-drinking good old boys with an open and forthright demeanor.*)

TREVIÑO: Hey, Epigmenio (*Simultaneously*): GARZA: Listen here, Estrella.

GUZMAN: Gentlemen, this falls in my jurisdiction, and that's that.

CESAR (*who has been watching them*): Whatever your business may be, gentleman, why don't you have a seat? (*Gesturing towards the members of his family.*) My wife and children.

(*The visitors greet them in silence except for ESTRELLA who, walks smiling up to ELENA, JULIA and MIGUEL while muttering inane pleasantries. He is clearly a low middle class city slicker. In the meantime, Epigmenio GUZMAN has been observing CESAR very closely.*)

GUZMAN: We need to discuss a very private matter. It would be preferable... (*Looking at the family.*)

CESAR: Elena…

(*ELENA takes JULIA by the hand and starts to leave. MIGUEL remains, in place looking alternately at his father and at the visitors.*)

ESTRELLA: Not in the least. Our business has to be conducted in absolute secrecy, but it does not exclude Señor Rubio's family. (*ELENA and JULIA have turned around.*)

SALINAS: The presence of the ladies is not essential for now.

TREVIÑO: This is men's business, my friend.

CESAR (*with a touch of irony, in reality somewhat uneasy due to MIGUEL's tense watchfulness and ELENA's anguish*): If it is on my account, gentlemen, you need not worry. I keep nothing from my family.

GARZA: Let's get down to business, then. You…

ESTRELLA: Mister representative, sir, please be reminded that I have been commissioned by the Party to clear this matter. In my opinion, Mrs. Rubio and Miss Rubio, who represent the Mexican family, should stay.

CESAR: Gentlemen, please have a seat. (*They all find their places, still arguing among themselves, except for GUZMAN who is still absorbed watching CESAR.*) Sir? (*To GUZMAN.*)

GUZMAN (*startled*): Thank you.

(*ESTRELLA and SALINAS end up sitting on the couch; GARZA and TREVIÑO sit on the armchairs, one on each side. At CESAR's prompting GUZMAN goes to sit on the couch leaving ESTRELLA sitting in the middle. ELENA and JULIA sit down at the other end of the room, facing the group of men. In order to see his father's face MIGUEL positions himself leaning against the arches; CESAR has his back to the audience. Looking more like someone who is on trial CESAR ends up in the foreground, right, facing the group of politicians.* The representatives look at GUZMAN and ESTRELLA.)

SALINAS: So, what is it going to be? Who is going to speak?

TREVIÑO: That's right. Who?

ESTRELLA (*beating GUZMAN to it*): Gentlemen... (*Clears his throat.*) His Excellency the President of the Republic and the National Revolutionary Party have instructed me to investigate Professor Bolton's revelations and to establish the identity of his source. Mr. Rubio, do you have anything to say? I want you to understand that our intentions are nothing but friendly.

CESAR (*slowly, feeling MIGUEL's intensely piercing gaze*): You are too young, gentlemen...... you are part of the revolutionary process of today. You cannot be expected, then, to recognize me. I have told you that I am Cesar Rubio. Is that all you want to know?

SALINAS (*to ESTRELLA*): My father knew General Cesar Rubio ... but he's dead now.

TREVIÑO: I had an uncle .... who served under him. He used to tell me about General Rubio. He's also dead.

GARZA: But there are still old men who could help identify him.

ESTRELLA: Dear colleagues, this is not getting us anywhere. (*To CESAR.*) My responsibility is to ascertain if you are General Cesar Rubio, if you have documents to prove that.

CESAR (*keenly aware of the fact that GUZMAN continues to observe him in silence*): If you have read the papers, and I am assuming that you did, you would know that I passed those documents on to Professor Bolton.

ESTRELLA: But, General, sir, er .... Mister Rubio, this is something of utmost importance. It's time for you to talk to us.

CESAR (*almost cornered*): Gentlemen. it was never my intention to revive the past...

MIGUEL (*taking two steps diagonally across the room, in front of his father*): Father, it is absolutely crucial that you start talking.

CESAR (*struggling*): What for?

ESTRELLA: Surely you understand that this revelation will carry a commanding weight in the political destiny of this country. All I ask of you, in the name of the President, in the name of the Party, in the name of the nation, is a document. I reiterate to you that our intentions are nothing but friendly. Just give us proof.

CESAR (*raising his head*): There are things, sir, that do not need any proof. What purpose does it serve to investigate my life? Why don't you just leave me alone in my little corner of the world?

ESTRELLA: Because if you are General Cesar Rubio you don't belong to yourself. You belong to the Revolution, to a loving motherland who has always cared for her heroes.

SALINAS: Wait a minute. Before you start giving speeches, Señor Estrella, we'd like for him to identify himself.

GARZA: Let him identify himself... (*Simultaneously*) TREVIÑO: That's all we are asking.

MIGUEL: Father... (*Takes one more step towards him*).

CESAR: Strange, isn't it, that those who need material proof should be precisely people from around here.... (*Looking at MIGUEL.*) and my son. (*MIGUEL takes one step back and lowers his head.*) Why don't you just let me stay dead?

ESTRELLA (*his mind made up*): I can understand your decision, General; speaking for the national Revolutionary Party and for myself I can assure you that further proof will not be necessary. I am certain that the President will not need it either; all we need...

SALINAS (*standing up*): But we do.

ESTRELLA: Allow me. It's the people, the press; it won't be long before they get here. (*CESAR and ELENA exchange glances.*) It's the bureaucrats in the Department of Defense, it won't be long before they too get here. Why don't you trust in us and give us that small proof? That way we can tell the people that we stand by you.

CESAR: The people are the only ones who do not need any proof. They follow their instinct, and that's enough for them. I refuse to identify myself to you.

MIGUEL: But why, father?

GARZA: No need to take offense, General. We are here on a peace mission. If we ask for proof it's for your own benefit.

SALINAS: The best thing to do now is to bring some old man from the town. I'll go in the car.

TREVIÑO: We ask for proof as an act of good faith.

ESTRELLA: I feel that the General is right. (*To CESAR.*) You may have noticed that I haven't begrudged you the rank of general, which is rightfully yours. (*To the others.*) But if he knew the reason why we are here, he would understand our insistence.

CESAR (*looking alternately to MIGUEL, and ELENA*): What is the purpose of your visit, then?

ESTRELLA: And that is the question, General. Let's give each other proof of our mutual trust.

CESAR (*feeling more confident*): You go first, then.

ESTRELLA (*smiling*): We are in the majority, General. These days the majority rules.

SALINAS: As far as we are concerned, if he refuses to identify himself, what do we care? He stays dead for us. It's as simple as that.

ESTRELLA: My mission and my interests are more far-reaching than yours, my dear colleagues.

TREVIÑO: Suit yourself… who cares about the authorities. We don't have much time to waste. Let's go, boys. (*They get up.*)

GARZA (*he stands up*): Wait a minute.

SALINAS (*getting up*): I always said that it was nothing but wishful thinking.

ESTRELLA (*standing up*): General, the military authorities could pressure you. Why do you persist in being this way? Why don't you name someone who knows you that can identify you? It's for your own good… for the good of the nation… and of its government. (*Turning around to face the family.*) But we are wasting our time. With due respect for your opinion, General, I am sure that you have powerful reasons to take such a position… maybe Mrs. Rubio could…

(*ELENA stands up.*)

CESAR (*forcefully, but with growing anxiety*): I want you to leave my wife out of this.

ELENA: That's alright, Cesar. It's got to be done. I'll testify.

CESAR: My wife knows nothing about this. (*To ELENA*) Be quiet.

GUZMAN (*speaking for the first time*): Just a minute. (*They all turn around; he is still sitting down.*) I've heard that Cesar Rubio would never forget a face. I'm not very good with faces but I can still remember his. I was still very young and I saw him only once; as far as I'm concerned, it's him. I've been watching you ever since I came in. (*Growing expectation.*) Perhaps you can remember my father, he served under you. (*He takes out an old railroad man's pocket watch and opens the back of it; he gets up and hands it over to CESAR.*) Do you recognize him?

CESAR (*he moves to wards the center of the stage. holding the watch in his hand while the rest of the men surround him looking on with curiosity . He hesitates before looking at the picture, looks at it and smiles. He raises his head and returns the watch to GUZMAN. Putting his hands in his pocket he sits on the couch saying*): Thank you.

GUZMAN: Do you know who he is? (*He moves closer.*)

CESAR (*slowly*): It's Isidro Guzman; he was killed by the huertistas in 1913, in Saltillo.

GUZMAN (*speaking to the others*): Don't you see, it's him

ESTRELLA: Are you, then, General Cesar Rubio?

SALINAS: That's no proof.

GUZMAN: Why did he recognize my old man, then?

TREVINO: No, no; that doesn't mean anything.

ESTRELLA: Just one moment, gentlemen. General, sir… I mean, Mister Rubio, where were you born? I hope that there is no problem sharing that information with me.

CESAR: Right here, in this town, when it was barely a village.

ESTRELLA: What street?

CESAR: There was only one street, then, Main Street.

ESTRELLA: What year?

CESAR: It was fifty years ago just this past July.

ESTRELLA (*takes a telegram out of his pocket and takes a quick look*): Thank you, General. I don't know how you feel about this, my friends, but that's proof enough for me. All the information checks out.

GUZMAN: Me too. He recognized my old man.

CESAR (*smiling*): They called him Old Coot.

GUZMAN (*excited*): That's him

CESAR (*driving the point home*): He was a brave man

GUZMAN (*more excited*): No question about it. That was my old man… he died fighting. Brave from the old school, like you, General.

CESAR: Which one? (*They laugh.*) No… the Old Coot died trying to protect Cesar Rubio. When the federal troops fired on Cesar, who was riding in front, Colonel Guzman reared his horse and blocked the way. They shot him, but he saved Cesar Rubio's life.

TREVIÑO: Why do you talk about yourself as if you were talking about somebody else?

CESAR (*gradually more in control*): Because maybe that's what has happened. Besides, that's what I do in the classroom… (*He gets up.*) Now, gentlemen, are you satisfied?

SALINAS: Well…. not quite.

GARZA: There's something else.

CESAR: And what would that be?

SALINAS (*looking to the others*): Papers, more proof, that's what we need.

CESAR (*after a pause*): I am sure that Professor Bolton will publish the documents I handed over to him, which is all I had. When you see that your curiosity will be satisfied. But until then, think of me as someone who is dead; just let me end my days in peace. I wanted to retire in my hometown, but I could go somewhere else.

(*Excitement and objections among the politicians. Even SALINAS and GARZA find themselves objecting. The entire family has drawn closer to CESAR. After much effort, making faces and waving his arms ESTRELLA succeeds in making himself heard.*)

ESTRELLA: General, sir, if I have come here representing the National Revolutionary Party and on a personal mission representing the President himself, it has not been out of mere curiosity or just to pester you with requests for proof of identity.

GUZMAN: Same here. I came as the mayor of Allende to discuss matters of public interest. The state representatives came with the same purpose.

GARZA: That's true.

CESAR (*looking at ELENA*): What is it that you want, then?

ELENA (*walking towards the group*): I know what they are after... they want to get you involved in politics. Tell them you are not interested, Cesar.

ESTRELLA: That wonderful feminine intuition. General, sir, your wife is a very intelligent woman.

SALINAS: Treviño.

TREVINO: What is it?

(*SALINAS drags TREVIÑO by the arm and takes him to the door, where, they carry on what is supposed to be a private conversation. GUZMAN watches them, shaking his head.*)

GUZMAN (*looking at SALINAS and TREVIÑO*): The lady has hit the nail on the head.

SALINAS (*slowly, in a low voice, not audible to the audience, as GUZMAN speaks*): Go to the town as fast as you can. Take the car. (*TREVIÑO nods in the affirmative.*).

(*It is absolutely essential that the actors utter these words in a way that makes it impossible for the audience to hear. Having them say these words suggests a planned activity; it also avoids an interruption in the flow of the action while allowing the actors to remain in character as long as they are on the stage.*)

CESAR: Thank you. Is that, then, what you are after?

ESTRELLA: General, we are not interested in short-term political gain. Your reappearance is truly provident... (*He corrects himself, stop-*

ping to look for the right word.), truly propitious and revolutionary…

(*Meanwhile, still saying the words in a way that cannot be heard by the audience.*)

SALINAS: …and bring Emeterio Rocha.

ESTRELLA: …and the timing could not be better. This state, as you well know, is about to elect a new governor.

SALINAS (*same as above*): He knew Cesar Rubio. Understand?

TREVIÑO (*same thing*): I see. Now I see what you're saying.

CESAR (*to ESTRELLA*): I am aware of that… but it doesn't have anything to do with me.

SALINAS (*same as above, slapping TREVIÑO on the shoulder*): OK, then? Just to make sure. (*TREVIÑO nods in the affirmative.*) Go ahead and go.

(*TREVIÑO leaves quickly after looking around the room.*)

ESTRELLA: I'll have to disagree with you. General, sir… Your reappearance makes you the ideal candidate for governor of your home state.

ELENA: Cesar, no!

JULIA: But, mother, why not? Father deserves that.

(*She looks at him devotedly.*)

CESAR: That's right, why not? (*SALINAS joins the group, smiling.*) Let me explain this to you, Mister…

ESTRELLA: Rafael Estrella, at your command, General.

CESAR: What you need to understand, Mister Estrella. (*In character, without realizing it, already embodying the myth of CESAR RUBIO.*)

I stepped out of the political arena for ever. I'd rather continue leading the same humble and obscure life as before

ESTRELLA: But, General Rubio, with all due respect, you have no right to deprive the nation of your valuable contribution.

GUZMAN: The government is suffering from severe stagnation... you can change that.

CESAR: No. Cesar Rubio did his part by starting the revolution. I am old now. Others can carry it forward. Señor Estrella, are you saying this in an official capacity?

ESTRELLA: When I make you this offer, I do so as the official envoy from the National Revolutionary Party and the President of the Republic.

GUZMAN: I know how people feel in this part of the country, General. We all know that Navarro would continue the dirty business that is so typical of the current governor; they would do it together, and we are sick and tired of that. Navarro has a dubious reputation.

ESTRELLA: They know who you are and that's all they want to know. The Party, as the political entity responsible for safeguarding the integrity of the electoral process regards your reappearance as an opportunity for honest and fair political competition among the contestants for the governorship. Without ignoring the qualities of Mister Navarro, the likely candidate for the position, the Party prefers that the voting public be offered the opportunity to choose between two candidates, for the greater glory of the democratic process.

GUZMAN: The truth is, General, you' would win by a landslide.

GARZA: You can't say no. What do you think, Salinas, my friend?

SALINAS (*smiling*): A man of Cesar Rubio's stature, who contributed more than anyone to the revolution, cannot say no.

CESAR (*hesitant*): That's true; but he can refuse precisely because he did his part. The young, today's revolutionaries, need to do theirs.

ELENA: You're right, Cesar. You shouldn't even think about it.

JULIA: But don't you see, Mother? Father could become the governor! Father, you have to accept.

GUZMAN: Governor… who knows what next! All of the North would be behind him. (*CESAR shows that he realizes the seriousness of his dilemma.*)

ELENA (*understanding clearly what is happening*): Cesar, listen. Don't listen to them… you shouldn't…

MIGUEL: Why not, mother? (*Relentless.*)

ELENA: Cesar!

CESAR (*to GUZMAN*): Why did you say that? I never thought… Cesar Rubio did not join the revolution with the idea of becoming president.

GUZMAN: But I have thought about it, General. I thought about it the moment I heard the news about you.

ESTRELLA: The President of the Republic told me over the telephone; tell Cesar Rubio that I have always admired his revolutionary qualities, that in his reappearance I see a triumph for the revolution; tell him to throw his hat in as a pre-candidate and ask him to come and see me.

CESAR (*caught off guard*): No, no, no… I can't accept.

GUZMAN: You have to do it, General, sir.

GARZA: Do it for your state.

ESTRELLA: General, for the Revolution.

SALINAS (*smiling persistently*): Knowing what I know about Cesar Rubio, he would accept.

CESAR (*accepting the challenge*): The representative still has his doubts

about my identity. What he doesn't know is that Cesar Rubio was never drawn to the revolution by the mere ambition to rule. Power destroys a man's sense of self-worth. You are either a man, or you wield power. I'm just a man.

ESTRELLA: That's fine, General, but in Mexico only men rule.

GUZMAN: If you still have doubts, Salinas, you're not with us.

SALINAS: I am, but, to be completely honest, I don't want us to make a mistake. I have always been on the side of the winning party, and so have all of you. The General has not given us any proof so far… I'm not arguing; he has the right name; but, I don't want us to end up looking like fools… just in case… you know what I mean?

ESTRELLA: Salinas, my friend. I must confess to you that your attitude does not strike me as being very revolutionary.

CESAR: I can see the representative's point of view quite well… and he's right. We don't want anybody to end up looking like a fool… it might be best if we leave things as they are.

ELENA (*holding CESAR'S hand and squeezing it*): Thank you, Cesar.

(*He smiles, but it would be hard to explain why.*)

GUZMAN: See what you've done? (*SALINAS does not say anything.*) Don't worry about a thing, General. We'll take care of everything.

ESTRELLA: In my opinion, General, sir, you're not in a position to make any decision until you have spoken with his Excellency the President.

CESAR (looking *hopeless, finally drawn into the farce*): Should I? But if I did, it would be almost like accepting… .

ELENA: Write him a letter, Cesar; thank him, but don't go.

ESTRELLA: Madam, your husband, the General, displays scruples that do honor to him, but the Revolution must take precedent.

GUZMAN: General, sir, our state is going through a very difficult time. We all know what the governor is doing, we are aware of his shady deals and we don't accept any of it. We don't want Navarro; he is a man without scruples, devoid of any revolutionary spirit, he is an enemy of the people.

CESAR: Is he your enemy?

GUZMAN; That's not the issue. All the town councils are against them. In our last council of mayors we all voted for the impeachment of the governor; we are opposed to Navarro's candidacy.

SALINAS: The truth is the governor and Navarro are excluding all the good people in the region.

GARZA: They're too greedy; together they've swallowed the entire budget. They owe salaries to employees, teachers haven't been paid, nobody has been paid; but they have bought ranches and mansions for themselves.

CESAR: What you are saying is that neither the current governor nor General Navarro give you the opportunity to ... participate.

GUZMAN: Why fool ourselves? It's the truth, General. You can see right through it. What's the point of denying it?

ESTRELLA: The President sees in you a catalyst for positive change, someone who can reduce tension, who can pacify the region, someone capable of bringing harmony to the government of this state.

GARZA: But those of us who are from your home state see in you the fighter, the honest, man who symbolizes the spirit of the North. We don't see anything wrong with wanting to work with you. You aren't a thief or a criminal.

CESAR: Cesar Rubio never believed that the revolution should be fought on behalf of the North or in favor of the South, but for the entire nation.

ESTRELLA: All the more so, General. The spirit of unity and community that you express is the same that inspires the President towards his people.

ELENA (*close to CESAR*): Don't listen to them any more, Cesar. Tell them to go away... I beg you ...

CESAR (*pushes her aside. Pause*): Gentlemen, thank you so much but, in your enthusiasm, which by the way I very much admire, you have forgotten that there exists and insurmountable obstacle.

ESTRELLA: What do you mean, sir?

CESAR: The election will be held in less than a month.

GUZMAN: That's precisely why we'd like to settle things right now.

GARZA: The sooner the better.

SALINAS: Let's clear this up.

ESTRELLA: The news that came out in the papers, General, is the best publicity anyone could ask for. All you need to do to win the election, is submit your nomination.

CESAR: The obstacle I was referring to is of a constitutional nature.

GUZMAN: I'm not really sure what you are referring to, General, sir. We make it a habit to act in accordance with the Constitution.

CESAR (*smiling to himself*): In accordance with it, every candidate must have lived in the state for at least one year. I came back to my hometown only a month ago. (*He says this with a definitive tone of voice, almost triumphantly. It would be difficult, however, to tell what his ultimate goal is at this point.*)

GUZMAN: That's true, but...

SALINAS: I was aware of that, but I was waiting until the General would bring it up. His attitude removes all my doubts and convinces me that we should be looking for another candidate.

GARZA (*shyly*): I am sure that a solution can be found, don't you think?...

ESTRELLA: I must inform you that the Party is regarding this political situation as an exceptional case... , almost as an emergency. The important thing is to rescue this state from its stagnation and to save it from the influence of reactionaries. The state constitution could also be subject to either an exception or an amendment.

SALINAS: Don't forget, my friend, that is a prerogative of the legislature.

ESTRELLA: I am perfectly aware of that, Mister Representative; the Party has taken this into account and is now counting on your support to see to it that the state constitution is, in fact, amended.

SALINAS: That remains to be seen.

GUZMAN: Hold on, Salinas.

ESTRELLA: I don't believe that this is the time and the place to argue...

CESAR (*calmly*): There are precedents, aren't there? The federal constitution has been amended for political reasons in cases involving reelection and term extensions. And it happens more frequently in the case of state constitutions.

SALINAS: Not in our state. You, are from the north, you should know that.

CESAR (*calmly*): When, for example, a candidate has occupied positions of high responsibility in the federal government, he has been exempted from the requirement of living in his home state for an entire year before the election. All he has needed to do is to pay a few visits. But...

ESTRELLA: Certainly, General Rubio. Governments cannot afford to rule themselves by laws of a general nature, laws that do not make room for exceptions. The Party will do now what it has done in the past.

CESAR: Except that I do not fit any of those categories. What made me leave my home state was not a position of responsibility in the federal government but a humble appointment as a professor of history of the revolution.

GUZMAN: That seems to me to have even more merit.

ESTRELLA: General, sir, let the Party take care of the legal aspects of the situation. We have resolved problems that have been far more complicated; so it is up to you now, we could leave tonight for Mexico City

CESAR (*directing his comment to SALINAS*): The state legislature would not oppose this, would they?

GARZA: Pardon me General, but Mister Salinas here is not the state legislature; he is no Luis XIV either.

CESAR (*to SALINAS*): Well, what do you have to say?

SALINAS: When I see you all so enthusiastic about this and so confident I don't know what to say. But, if necessary, I will still oppose it in the House.

ESTRELLA: Señor Salinas, my dear friend, don't you think that your situation is very similar to that of the General? Quite unintentionally, of course; I remember that your election to the House was arranged by you in Mexico City, wasn't it.

SALINAS (*with conviction*): It's not the same thing. I was on an official assignment in the capital.

ESTRELLA: But it is exactly the same situation with our General. The President is summoning him; that in itself constitutes an official assignment.

SALINAS: In that case I will just submit to the will of the majority.

ESTRELLA: You are a good revolutionary man, my friend. Those who are in the majority will appreciate your good disposition.

(*He extends his hand out to him with utmost insincerity.*)

ELENA (*anguished*): I've always hated politics, Cesar. Don't make me ...leave you.

CESAR: Gentlemen, my situation, as you can see, is a difficult one. My wife and I don't want to...

ESTRELLA: General, sir, the conflict between the public arena and a man's private life is a problem that may never be solved. But, a man like you cannot have a private life. That's the price you have to pay for your greatness and your heroism.

CESAR: Elena, do you think that I am too old to govern? You know my ideas, my dreams... you know that I could do some good for my home state, for my country... I could serve my country as well as any Mexican... .

GUZMAN: Oh, far better, General.

CESAR: Perhaps, deep down I've always wished for this opportunity. If they offer it to me freely, why can't I accept it? I'm an honest man. I could do some good. I've dreamed about the chance to do that for such a long time. If they think that I...

SALINAS: General, sir, what you've done for the revolution, your legacy is common knowledge. Nobody has any doubt about your ability to govern. Isn't that true, gentlemen?

GUZMAN: Of course. Nobody has any doubt that you will save our state.

GARZA: We're absolutely certain of it. In fact, we're counting on you.

ESTRELLA: The Party will make sure that someone like you, who has been away from public life for some time can count on the most reliable counsel. Isn't that so, Señor Salinas?

SALINAS: You can count on that Señor Estrella.

CESAR: Elena, try to understand what I want. Why not, Elena? You know that I wouldn't do anything without you.

ESTRELLA: The President, who's a good family man himself, will appreciate your noble gesture. You, Madam, must certainly remember the heroism and sacrifice of so many Mexican women. Use the heroines of our independence for inspiration. Or, better yet, use the soldaderas, *our* revolution's heroines.

ELENA (*with an almost aggressive gesture*): I beg of you, don't involve me in your tricks.

MIGUEL (*eagerly*): There's something you are not telling us, Mother. Why? What is it?

JULIA: Mother, I understand very well... you're afraid. But you can help Father.... perhaps I can, too.

MIGUEL: What is it, Mother?

JULIA: Leave her alone, stop torturing her with those questions. Mother...

ELENA: Cesar!

CESAR (*looking at her squarely and speaking slowly*): Say what you have to say. Go ahead and do it.

ELENA: I'm afraid for you, Cesar.

ESTRELLA: Madam, we are all responsible for the General's life, but his best protection is his own glorious destiny.

ELENA: Cesar!

CESAR (*impatient, now with cold finality*): Go ahead and say it! Say it!

(*ELENA stands up, wringing her hands. At the very moment when she is about to scream the truth TREVIÑO and EMETERIO ROCHA appear at the door, right. ROCHA is a strong, healthy old man, about sixty five years of age. They all turn towards them.*)

TREVINO: Which one is it?

SALINAS: Can you recognize him, old man?

ROCHA (*stops, looks around*): Which one, did you say? This one? (*Takes a step towards CESAR.*)

CESAR (*he moves forward after one last hint at the possibility of flight: now it is all or nothing*):: Don't you remember me, Emeterio Rocha?

ROCHA (*looking at him carefully*): It's been so many years…

GUZMAN: The General did recognize him.

SALINAS: But, that's not the issue.

ROCHA: I don't think you've changed very much. You grew a mustache, though. You're still the same.

SALINAS: What's his name, old man?

CESAR: Go on, Emeterio, say it.

ROCHA (*struggling to remember*): Well, I guess, it's strange. But you are the same… why, yes. You are Cesar Rubio…

CESAR: Are you sure that it is my name, Emeterio?

ROCHA: I couldn't call you by any other name. Of course, Cesar… Cesar Rubio. I know you from when you used to play marbles on Main Street.

CESAR: Are you sure you recognize me?

ROCHA (*simply, holding his hand out to him*): Didn't they say that you were dead, Cesar?

(*CESAR shakes his hand, smiling.*)

TREVIÑO: There's a crowd outside. (*Gradually, the sound of voices can be heard.*)

GUZMAN: That's it. The whole town knows now. Alright, Salinas. No more doubts now.

MIGUEL (*looking at CESAR*): That's it?

SALINAS: That's it. I'm sorry, General, sir. (*CESAR shakes his hand without saying anything. The voices become louder and clearer. They say: Cesar Rubio! We want Cesar Rubio!*)

ESTRELLA: General, sir, all you have to do is say the word, say that you accept.

ELENA: Cesar...

CESAR (*with dignity*): If you feel that I can do some good, I accept. I gratefully accept.

(*JULIA kisses him. ELENA looks at him anxiously and squeezes his hand. MIGUEL takes a step back.*)

GUZMAN (*runs to the door, right and yells toward the outside*): Viva Cesar Rubio! Hurray for Cesar Rubio! (*Loud voices within: Viva! Hurray! The women run to the window; they look outside.*)

JULIA: Look, Father, look! (*CESAR moves closer.*) That man with the black mustache is the man who came looking for you a few days ago.

ESTRELLA (*also looking*): Do you know him, General?

CESAR (*after a pause*): He is the so-called general, Navarro.

ROCHA: He served under you. I believe he was your assistant, wasn't he? But, once a thief...

(*CESAR remains silent. Voices in the wings: Cesar Rubio! Cesar Rubio! Cesar Rubio!*)

GUZMAN (*coming in*): General, out there, please. They want to see you.

ESTRELLA (*looking out and rubbing his hands*): The press is here too.

(*CESAR walks towards the door. MIGUEL blocks his way.*)

CESAR: What do you want? (*MIGUEL does not give an answer.*) So, it seems like you don't believe any of this, do you?

MIGUEL: Do you?

ESTRELLA and THE CROWD: Viva Cesar Rubio! Long live our hero!

CESAR (*with one gesture*) This is my response.

(*He exits. MIGUEL walks up to ELENA and holds her hand, in silence. More cheering can be heard outside.*)

THE VOICE OF THE PHOTOGRAPHER: Hold it one moment, General. (*Flash.*) Now one shaking Señor Estrella's hand. That's perfect! (*Flash.*) Now with the family. (*Cheering.*)

CESAR (*sticking his head in*): Come here, Elena; come, Julia, Miguel. (*ELENA comes closer, he holds her by the waist and squeezes her.*) Everything, with you! (*Exit all. JULIA follows them. More cheering within.*)

(*MIGUEL remains alone, with his back towards the door and the window to the right; he walks towards the front, center stage. From there he walks back to the door. The noise is deafening.*)

CESAR'S VOICE (*within*): Miguel. Son!

(*MIGUEL storms out to the left with a violent gesture of disgust while the sound of voices and of firecrackers or gunfire can be heard outside.*)

CURTAIN.

Palacio de Bellas Artes

HOY

EL GESTICULADOR

OBRA DE

RODOLFO USIGLI

★

(Left) Cover of program for the May 17, 1947 premiere of *El gesticulador* at the Palacio de Bellas Artes in Mexico City. (Rodolfo Usigli Archive, Miami University Libraries, Oxford, Ohio).

(Bottom) Alfredo Gómez de la Vega, extreme right, in the role of César Rubio. (Rodolfo Usigli Archive, Miami University Libraries, Oxford, Ohio).

ACT THREE

(A month later, about 11 o'clock in the morning, in Professor Cesar Rubio's house. The living room looks now more like a temporary office. There is a desk, a typing table, a typewriter; piles of papers and books. Next to the arches, by the dining room, on the ground, there is a roll of posters. One of them, half unrolled, shows Cesar Rubio's face with the caption: The People's Candidate. The general atmosphere of improvisation and disarray of the room creates the appearance of poverty; this is an attempt at satisfying Cesar Rubio's *insistence on giving a false impression of modesty.*

Sitting at the desk, ESTRELLA is now answering the mail. GUZMAN is sitting on the couch, smoking a cigarette. SALINAS, also smoking, is leaning against the door on the right.)

ESTRELLA: Gentlemen, this is a telegram from the President. *(The others turn around, he reads.)* "Best wishes to you during today's election. Stop. May the people recognize you as a hero of the Revolution. Stop. Should the result be different, be assured that your contribution will still be regarded as invaluable. Stop. Please report election result immediately. Stop. Cordially yours." *(He puts down the telegram.)* This is truly an historical document, one of a kind.

GUZMAN: There's no way we'd lose this election, even if the president didn't support us. Such a groundswell of popular support had not been seen since the election of Madero. The General has won everybody over.

ESTRELLA: He is such an extraordinary man. He is a good listener, a man of a few words, he only says what is strictly necessary; he acts with an energy and openness that I'd never seen before. We shouldn't neglect, however, the support of centrist forces. Isn't that right, Mr. Salinas? *(SALINAS nods.)* He had no trouble winning the President over. You've seen how well he is doing here.

SALINAS: In my entire political experience, I've never seen anything like it. The election is practically decided; still, I have a strange feeling about it.

GUZMAN: There you go again. No wonder everybody calls you Mister You Never Know.

ESTRELLA: What do you mean by that?

SALINAS *(moves away from the door crossing to the foreground center)*: I mean, there are lots of nasty rumors circulating. In any case, Navarro is not the type of man who is going to sit still. We have to be very careful; maybe the General should start carrying a gun, just in case.

GUZMAN: Didn't I tell you? You would probably talk him out of running instead of carrying a gun. Listen, Salinas, my friend: he is not like you and me. Besides, I have organized an excellent security system. You have nothing to worry about.

SALINAS: I hope you're right. I am also convinced that he is an exceptional individual, there's nobody like him, and he should help us fulfill our greatest dreams. But, Epigmenio, it is absolutely essential that nothing happens to him.

GUZMAN: You worry too much, my friend!

ESTRELLA *(getting up):* Our friend Salinas here suffers from what the French call an *ideé fixe (They look at each other.)* It means: a fixed idea. I wish you would tell us what you mean. The voting process is supposed to start at 11:30... *(Looks at his watch.)* We don't have much time to get there. Well, dear friend, what is it?

SALINAS: In the first place, Navarro said that General Rubio will not win as long as he is around. *(GUZMAN makes mocking sound.)* ... he also... *(He stops.)*

GUZMAN: What is it? Go ahead and say it.

SALINAS: He said that he... he can prove that General Rubio is an impostor. *(He wipes his forehead off. GUZMAN breaks out laughing boisterously.)*

ESTRELLA: I believe I need to have a few words with General Navarro in the name of the Party.

GUZMAN: Hey, Salinas, he's worse than you.

SALINAS: The moment Naverro opens his mouth people will know he's lying. Just in case, though, we need to be on the look out.

ESTRELLA: Do you want my honest opinion, gentlemen?

GUZMAN: Let's hear it.

ESTRELLA: If General Navarro could take a closer look at General Rubio, the same would happen to him as it did with others, which is what happened to you, Salinas.

SALINAS: And what would that be?

ESTRELLA: He would become a Rubista *(The others laugh.)* I'm serious. General Rubio has this magnetism that is so hard to explain. I know, for example, how difficult a man the head of the party is. Well, they hadn't spent more than half an hour together before Rubio had him eating out of his hand. *(GUZMAN laughs with satisfaction.)*

SALINAS: Where's Garza? Wasn't he supposed to be back by 10:30?

GUZMAN: Garza is there, making all the necessary arrangements. We'll see him there.

SALINAS: What about Treviño?

ESTRELLA: He's there helping Garza.

SALINAS: But they should be back by now, shouldn't they?

GUZMAN: Relax, don't be so nervous! It's not like you're the candidate.

ESTRELLA: That's what happens to the bridesmaids at a wedding. They get overly anxious.

SALINAS: You can joke all you want. I won't rest until I see the General in the governor's office. Just in case.

GUZMAN: Be quiet. He's coming.

(CESAR's steps can be heard on the stairs. The three men gather to welcome him. CESAR RUBIO comes in. He has experienced an incredible transformation in the last few weeks. The frenzied outbursts, the controlled nervous energy, the fevered ambition, the struggle against fear have given his features a noble serenity and his gaze a clarity of vision and an overall appearance of incredible self-assurance. He looks pale and gaunt but he carries himself with the quiet dignity that is so typical in a peasant of some distinction. Despite the heat, he is wearing a pair of trousers and a jacket made of dark cashmere, a good quality white shirt and a navy blue cotton tie. He is carrying in his hand a Texas-style broad-brimmed white hat that bears a five-star general insignia. The hat could be construed as the only concession to luxury in his new identity, if we were not to consider, in the first place, a new level of fastidious cleanliness and attention to personal care in his general appearance.)

CESAR: Good morning, gentlemen.

ALL: Good morning, General, sir.

ESTRELLA; How is his Excellency, the Governor, today?

CESAR: Let's not rush things, Estrella. There is no harm in waiting.

GUZMAN: The election is as good as won, sir.

ESTRELLA: General, sir, if you have any doubts, just take a look at this telegram from the President.

CESAR *(after taking a quick look at the telegram)*: No doubt whatsoever, Estrella. When a person knows how things are supposed to be or not supposed to be there cannot be any room for doubt. *(He puts his hat down on the desk and he pushes the telegrams aside with his hand without paying much attention to them,)* The best part about being a politician... Did we get a telegram from Professor Bolton?

ESTRELLA: He sends his congratulations, General, but he says that he cannot come. He will be able to attend your inauguration, though.

CESAR *(simply)*: I would have liked to see him sooner. *(He walks from one end of the room to the other, slowly.)* The best part about being a politician is that it puts you in contact with the source of everything, with the facts, the action. Politics is very much like a syntax of life, something that connects everything. But what I really prefer is that it forces you to live face to face with the passing of time, without any possibility of escape, to walk hand in hand with time without wasting a second. *(He stops, picks up the poster and takes a look at it. He, then, looks around for a place to hang it, while talking. GUZMAN and SALINAS rush headlong, grab the poster and hang it from one of the arches. CESAR takes a look at himself as he continues talking.)* It helps you look deep into human passion more directly without any waste of time. It allows you to see at first sight that everything has a price... which you have to pay. Politics puts you in close contact with the root causes, with the web of interconnected systems that control all movement, even that of the stars. You come to understand the cause and the purpose of everything; but you know also that you cannot tell anyone. You discover the price of every person. Thus, the great politician becomes the pulse, the very heart of everything.

ESTRELLA *(the only one to have understood some of it)*: As a matter of fact, General, politics is superior to everything else. It summons a person's entire body and spirit.

CESAR *(ignoring the interruption)*: The politician is the axle of a wheel, which is the people; when the axle breaks or decays, the wheel comes apart. The politician separates what is not meant to be together, he harnesses forces and elements that cannot function in isolation. At the beginning, the human forces that spin around the political leader produce a sensation of emptiness and death; after, he realizes that he performs a function, in that the movement, the rhythm of the wheel cannot occur without the axle, without him. Then, he can experience the inner peace of power, which comes from the ability to generate energy and to propel others harmoniously in time. Can you see any resemblance to me in that poster?

GUZMAN: Certainly, I can see the resemblance. Just the other day, one of the old people in the town, someone who knew you from the start of the Revolution, upon seeing one of these posters said: Cesar hasn't changed a bit; he looks the same as when they killed all his men in Hidalgo, 30 years ago.

ESTRELLA: General, heroism is like the perpetual patina of youth.

CESAR: That's so true. This portrait looks more like the Cesar Rubio of the start of the Revolution than me. And yet, it's me. *(He smiles.)* It's really strange. Who painted it?

SALINAS: An old engraver here in town.

CESAR: The people can understand so many things. *(He smiles. He opens his mouth as if about to add something. He checks himself, and takes a few steps with his hands behind his back.)* Did you make the necessary changes in the speech, Estrella?

ESTRELLA: It's ready, General.

CESAR: The way we had agreed... about my resurrection?

ESTRELLA: Yes, General. *(He recites)* "Only a noble, suffering people can expect events such as... "

CESAR *(interrupting him):* Can I have it, please. *(ESTRELLA hands it over.)* Are there any people outside?

GUZMAN: About 20 or 30.

CESAR: Salinas, go ahead and tell them that I'll see them at the polling station. *(SALINAS exits. CESAR finishes reading the text of the speech; he gives it back to ESTRELLA.)* That's very good, Estrella. *(Checks the time on his pocket watch.)*

ESTRELLA: Thank you, General

SALINAS *(returning)*: Sir, I believe it's time to go.

CESAR: Have the people left?

SALINAS: No. They all want to follow you into town. *(CESAR smiles.)* The cars are all ready.

CESAR: We'll head out shortly. Let me say goodbye to my wife. *(He heads toward the door, left. At that moment TREVIÑO comes in, breathless.)*

TREVIÑO: General, sir.

CESAR *(almost at the door, he turns around)*: What is it? *(The others gather closer together.)*

TREVIÑO: General, sir, here comes Navarro. He's coming to see you.

CESAR *(takes one more step forward)*: Navarro?

GUZMAN: He has the gall! What does he want here?

ESTRELLA: There's only one reason. He is here to strike a deal because the head of the party sent someone to talk some sense into him.

SALINAS: I'm not so sure. I don't trust him.

GUZMAN: What should we do, General?

CESAR: Let him come in. I am going to say goodbye to my wife. Tell him to wait for me right here.

TREVIÑO: But he probably wants to talk to you in private.

CESAR *(smiling)*: No doubt.

ESTRELLA: Are you going to let him see you?

CESAR: Why not?

SALINAS: General, sir, please... *(Draws his gun out and hands it over to him.)*

CESAR *(smiling)*: No, Salinas. Those scare me.

SALINAS *(pleading)*: General, sir...

CESAR *(patting him on the arm)*: That's silly. Put that away, Son.

GUZMAN: It doesn't matter, sir, we're all armed.

CESAR *(sternly):* Be very careful, Epigmenio. Navarro is here to negotiate. Don't do anything foolish. Bring him in, exercise caution, be polite with him and to the people that he's with. *(Gestures of disapproval.)* I want you to follow my orders, understand? *(Goes back to the desk to fetch his hat)*

GUZMAN: Alright, General, we'll do as you say. *(CESAR exits left.)*

ESTRELLA *(smiling and raising his arms):* Gentlemen, that's one tough man.

GUZMAN: I don't care. If only this (*Pointing to his gun.)* would just go off by itself, when Navarro is here...

SALINAS *(to TREVIÑO)*: Who is with him?

TREVIÑO: I can't really tell from here, but I believe it's Salas and León.

GUZMAN: Those two are packing guns for sure. I have a bad feeling about this. Something is going to happen here.

ESTRELLA: Don't worry. Bet you anything that he withdraws his name from the election; he is here to ask for a job. Don't worry.

SALINAS *(laughing)*: That's too easy! Mr. Estrella, you still don't know us northerners very well, do you. *(Goes to the door.)*

ESTRELLA: He'd get better results that way; it could even give him a better standing within the Party.

GUZMAN: We'll just have to keep our eyes peeled.

SALINAS *(from the door)*: They're here. *(Reenters.)*

(Without saying anything GUZMAN, TREVIÑO and SALINAS check their guns; they make sure that they can draw from their holsters without any problem and wait lined up looking towards the door.)

ESTRELLA *(as he speaks, he positions himself surreptitiously right behind them)*: You are taking unnecessary precautions, gentlemen. Besides, you take an offensive posture against the General's orders.

GUZMAN *(clenching his teeth, without turning around)*: How do we know what to expect from them?

SALINAS *(without turning around)*: This is just in case.

TREVIÑO *(same thing)*: Maybe what happens here is what should have happened a long time ago.

GUZMAN *(without turning. With a chuckle)*: I've had my eye on Navarro for quite some time now.

ESTRELLA *(making certain that he is well covered, as he looks toward the door)*: Careful! Be careful! Gentlemen, we have to obey the General's orders...

(They all watch the door very intently; after a moment they relax. TREVIÑO is the first one to sit down, without saying anything.)

GUZMAN *(wiping his forehead off and walking towards the couch)*: Psh. Let them come whenever they feel like it.

SALINAS *(rolling a cigarette and lowering his guard)*: You fellows get tired pretty quickly.

ESTRELLA *(returning to the desk)*: It's better this way, you know.

(At that exact moment, as if he had been waiting for a change in their mood, NAVARRO enters with one gunman at each side. It's the STRANGER from Act Two.)

NAVARRO: So, how are you all doing, fellas? *(Collective shock. They all stand up and gather together.)* Don't be scared. *(Crosses to the center.)* Where is that little professor. *(Laughing.)* You were not expecting me, huh?

ESTRELLA *(a bit shaky but with some composure)*: General Rubio already knows that you are here; he would like for you to please wait for him.

(NAVARRO's men are mildly amused by the formality.)

NAVARRO *(biting his lip)*: Alright, then. *(Turning to his bodyguards.)* So, looks like we'll have to wait, boys. What do you think?

SALAS: Like we had to at the presidential palace. *(He chuckles.)*

LEON *(imitating him)*: Whatever you want, Epignemio. How about this one? *(Motions as if to draw.)*

ESTRELLA: Gentlemen! Gentlemen!

NAVARRO: Hold it, León. *(EPIGMENIO GUZMAN and LEON retreat to opposite corners giving each other the ferocious look of two professional killers. To ESTRELLA.)* You are the party representative, aren't you. Tell Rubio that I want to talk with him, alone.

ESTRELLA: General Rubio knows that you wish to speak with him alone. It'll be as you wish.

NAVARRO *(biting his lip)*: No question that he is a professor, he knows everything. So, why don't you leave? What are you waiting for?

SALINAS: If you think that we are going to leave him here alone with three armed thugs.

NAVARRO (*threatening*): Watch it, Salinas... *(Transition, smiling.)* I'm not carrying a gun. See? *(He opens his jacket slightly to prove it.)*

GUZMAN: But they are.

NAVARRO: Salas, give your gun to him.

SALAS: But, listen...

NAVARRO *(growling):* Give him your gun. *(SALAS carries out the order begrudgingly.)* León, you wait for us in the car. Salas will go out in a few minutes, then you can wait for me together. *(After looking around at the others and spitting on the floor LEON exits.)* Now you, little wimps. It's your turn to hit the road. *(The others hesitate.)*

ESTRELLA: Gentlemen, the General gave strict orders.

GUZMAN *(to TREVIÑO)*: Come give me a hand. I have to watch this little pussycat here.

SALINAS: The General made it a point of saying that he wants to see Navarro, alone.

ESTRELLA: I'll go upstairs and I'll be back with the General. There's nothing to worry about.

NAVARRO: That's fine with me. Salas stays with me until the little professor gets here.

(GUZMAN and TREVIÑO exit. SALINAS follows them, shaking his head. Upon reaching the door he turns around showing his mistrust. ESTRELLA exits, left. He can be heard climbing the stairs.)

NAVARRO *(out loud)*: These guys are really scared! I bet you anything that they are going to spy on us.

SALAS: I don't understand why you would want to talk with Rubio.

NAVARRO: They say that he is a good talker, that's why. *(Laughing.)* Do you have any cigarettes? Give me one, will you. *(SALAS moves closer and offers him one.)* Do you have a light? *(SALAS strikes a match and moves closer to light his cigarette. At this point both men are standing up front, stage center, almost at the edge of the apron of the stage.)* Is everything ready?

SALAS: Everything is ready, boss.

(SALINAS sticks his head in briefly. NAVARRO sees him and smiles. SALINAS disappears.)

NAVARRO: You know what to do then. If there's no deal, you take off in the small car and start working on the setup.

SALAS: How am I going to know?

NAVARRO *(after a pause. He laughs)*: You don't expect me to come out to give you the signal do you? But since his men are going to be on the lookout I'll make sure that Salinas comes back inside. A soon as you see him come in, you take off.

SALAS: Alright.

NAVARRO: I don't want anything to go wrong. As soon as the deed is done make sure that you get rid of that lunatic. Don't forget the cross and the scapular.

SALAS: That part is all set. Salinas is the signal, then.

NAVARRO: Yes, as soon as he comes in. If he does not come in, then just wait for me with León.

SALAS: Alright.

NAVARRO: You'd better go now. *(He laughs.)* Otherwise they're going to think that we are plotting something.

(SALAS exits right. NAVARRO looks around the room; upon seeing the poster he grins sarcastically. He walks up to it smiling, he stops, raises his hand and hits the image with the back of his hand. Steps can be heard on the stairs. NAVARRO turns around and waits expectantly. A moment later CESAR RUBIO and ESTRELLA walk in from the left. The two antagonists meet face to face, center stage. They size each other up with contempt. CESAR is the first one to speak.)

CESAR: So, Navarro, how are you doing?

NAVARRO: So, Cesar, how are you doing?

CESAR: Señor Estrella, please wait outside for me. We'll be leaving shortly. *(NAVARRO laughs between his teeth. After glancing quickly at them he exits. As soon as they are alone CESAR speaks.)* Won't you sit down?

NAVARRO: Why not.

(He walks up to the couch followed by CESAR. They sit down.)

CESAR; Well, what is it, then?

NAVARRO: Excuse me, Cesar but I can't help laughing.

CESAR *(haughtily):* I beg your pardon.

NAVARRO: Cesar Rubio's shoes are too big for you. I can't imagine how you had the gall to get involved in a farce like this.

CESAR: What do you mean?

NAVARRO: Your name is Cesar Rubio but that's about all you have in common with the General. I've known you all your life, Cesar, you've got to remember that.

CESAR: Even the old men of the town recognized me.

NAVARRO: Of course. They remember your face but when they try to call you by your name they have no choice but to call you Cesar Rubio. Bah! Let's not waste words. You don't fool me.

CESAR *(contemptuously)*: Is that all you had to say to me?

NAVARRO: I also wanted to tell you not to be such a fool, to tell you to get out of this while you can. *(CESAR remains silent.)* By the time you change your mind it might be too late. *(CESAR still unmoved.)* Politics is serious business, Cesar. This is not the University of Mexico. In the world of politics we break more than windows and burn more than firecrackers.

CESAR: What do you intend to do?

NAVARRO: I am going to denounce you. When everybody finds out that you are a fraud, that you are copying the gestures of a dead man…

CESAR: Imbecile! How can you ever hope to deny what everybody believes to be true. For anyone from the North I am Cesar Rubio. Take a look at that poster, for example. Notice that the person in it resembles both of us.

NAVARRO: I'm going to denounce you anyway.

CESAR: But why are you afraid to look at the poster? Go ahead and denounce me. Go ahead and try, try and tell the Indians that their Virgin of Guadalupe was invented by the Spanish authorities, try that and you'll find out. I am the one and only Cesar Rubio because that's what the people want, that's what they believe.

NAVARRO: You're nothing but a cheap impostor. And you have come up with the most absurd scheme. Up here you start acting like you are some kind of genius because nobody can challenge you. Then, you come up with the crazy idea that you are a general!

CESAR: Just like you.

NAVARRO: What was that?

CESAR: I'm saying what I'm doing is no different than what you've done. You are as much of a general as I am or anyone else. *(MIGUEL enters ever so slightly at that moment without having made any sound as he came down. Upon hearing the voices he stops, takes a step back and disappears without being seen; from this moment on he will stick his head in several times.)* How did you get to be a general? Cesar Rubio made you a lieutenant because you were good at stealing horses, but that's all. The old chief, you know who I'm talking about, made you a general because you helped kill all those Catholics. And that was not all… all the women you got for him. That's your military record.

NAVARRO *(seething with anger):* You're sticking your nose in things that…

CESAR: Isn't it true? Every night at police headquarters you would drink down a whole bottle of cognac so that you could personally execute the prisoners. And that was not all you had …

NAVARRO: Watch it!

CESAR: About what? I may not be the great Cesar Rubio, but who are you? What is each one of us in Mexico? Look around and all you see are impostors, impersonators, and simulators, fakes all of them. Killers disguised as heroes, rich fat cats disguised a leaders, thieves disguised as congressmen, government officials disguised as experts, political bosses disguised as true democrats, charlatans disguised as lawyers, demagogues disguised as men of good will. Does anyone call them into account? They are all a bunch of two-faced hypocrites.

NAVARRO: None of them has stolen, as you have, someone else's identity.

CESAR: Are you sure? They all steal other people's ideas; they are all fake like the bottles that are used in the theater: the label says cognac but they're full of lemonade; they're like radishes and watermelons: one color outside and another inside. It's part of the culture. It runs through our history, something you know nothing about. But, just take a closer look at yourself. You worked closely with all the political bosses in all the parties because you have done the same favors to all of them. Those who have remained above the fray have always needed you to commit their crimes, they have dumped onto you their remorse, like into a garbage can. Instead of squashing you like an insect, they have covered you with honors and money because you knew their secrets and did their dirty deeds.

NAVARRO *(with rage)*: It's got nothing to do with me; but with you, a mediocre two-bit professor, a failure of a man who couldn't do anything by himself, not even kill; someone who is able to live only by hiding behind the image of a dead man. That is worse than anything else. And you did it, the person I am about to denounce today; and to hold you up to ridicule if it is the last thing I do. There's still time for you to back out, Cesar. Get out of my way, don't push me.

CESAR: And who are you that I should be afraid? I may not be Cesar Rubio, *(MIGUEL's face, showing with an anguished expression, can be seen briefly.)* but I know that I can be like him, do what he wanted to do. I know that I can do a lot of good for my country, stopping thieves and murderers like you from taking over... I know that I can come up with better ideas to run this country in one day than you could possibly imagine in your entire life. You and your kind have shown your ineptitude, have demonstrated that you are rotten to the core; all you can do is add to Mexico's shame and hypocrisy. You know what else? You don't scare me. I started with a lie but I have become true to myself. I don't know how, but I no longer doubt myself! Now I know my destiny: I am convinced that my duty is to live out Cesar Rubio's destiny.

NAVARRO *(standing up)*: It's up to you, but don't complain later, because today everyone in this town, in the state and in the country is going to find out the truth about you.

CESAR *(standing up)*: Go ahead and denounce me. You couldn't come up with a better way to do yourself in.

NAVARRO: What is that supposed to mean?

CESAR: So, you're interested, huh? But, tell me one thing: how are you going to prove that I am not Cesar Rubio?

(MIGUEL reappears and hides his face in his hands.)

NAVARRO: You'll see.

CESAR: I'm too curious to wait. By the way, nobody will believe a word of what you'll say. You have a reputation for being a corrupt criminal; the people hate you too much to believe you. How are you going to prove that Cesar Rubio died in 1914?

NAVARRO: That's no problem.

CESAR: That's what I thought. You can go and prove anything you want. You may be able to destroy me, but you'll also destroy yourself.

NAVARRO: Explain yourself.

CESAR: What for? You are not as sure of yourself as you think.

NAVARRO: I am sure, so sure that I know today's the day I'll destroy you.

CESAR: Is that right? *(Takes a deep breath)* So, you say that you are going to prove beyond any doubt Cesar Rubio's death.

NAVARRO: Yes.

CESAR *(he sits down)*: If you knew any history, you'd know how difficult that would be.

NAVARRO: I'll prove it.

CESAR: You could do that only if you had witnessed his death.

NAVARRO: I did.

CESAR: Why didn't you try to save him then?

NAVARRO: It wasn't possible… there were too many of them.

CESAR: That was the official report they made up. You are lying.

NAVARRO: In the shoot out…

CESAR: There was no shoot out.

NAVARRO: What?

CESAR: There was only one killer and for the first time in his career he polished off a bottle of cognac so as to have a steady hand.

NAVARRO: That's not true! Not true!

CESAR: Why do you deny it before I even say anything?

NAVARRO *(somewhat shaky):* I haven't denied anything.

CESAR: You were too sure of yourself when you first saw me, the day all the townspeople came, four weeks ago. By the time I was leaving you looked like you were going to faint. It was all those doubts, the remorse, the fear…

NAVARRO: Me? Why should I? What a fool you are. You don't even know what you are saying.

CESAR *(standing up, with awesome majesty)*: You blinded Canales his assistant with one shot, remember?

NAVARRO: That's a lie!

CESAR: You killed Captain Solis; you always felt envious of him because he was Cesar Rubio's favorite.

NAVARRO: I'm telling you, that's a lie!

CESAR *(towering)*: You killed Cesar Rubio!

NAVARRO: No!

CESAR: You should have killed Canales or cut his tongue. He's alive and I know where he lives. They made you a colonel because of this crime.

NAVARRO: That's nothing but a slanderous lie! If you are so sure of that, why didn't you tell your American friend?

CESAR: Because I thought then that I was going to need you. But I don't. Go on and turn me in. I'll provide all the necessary proof, whatever is needed to show that you are telling the truth… it's the least I can do for an old friend. *(Overwhelmed, NAVARRO drops down in an armchair. CESAR looks at him and continues.)* You thought you had all the aces. What did you say to yourself? You said: This schoolteacher is a poor devil who is after his cut. I'll give him a good scare first, then I'll throw him a bone to chew on. Because, don't deny it, I have it on good authority: you had come to offer me the presidency of the state university. I'm sorry I can't offer it to you, after all, you can't even read or write. Now, let's go to the polls and see what happens, whatever it may be.

NAVARRO *(pulling himself together)*: Alright, if you turn me in, it's all over for you, too.

CESAR: I really don't care. You'll keep your mouth shut. My crime is nothing compared to yours, and I'm being generous. You have 24 hours to leave the country, you understand? You have plenty of money. With all you have stolen.

NAVARRO: I'm not leaving. I'd rather…

CESAR: If you choose to stay I'll prove that you tried to kill me and I will also show how I got away. I can do it; don't imagine for a moment that I did not expect to have this conversation with you. I've been waiting for you every day for a week now and I have taken the necessary precautions. *(He looks at his watch.)* It's time to go to the polls now.

NAVARRO; *(after an excruciating pause)*: As you wish, but I'm giving you fair warning that I, too, have taken some precautions, it would be best for you not to go to the polls.

CESAR: What do you know about fairness? The word should blow up in your face and tear you to pieces.

NAVARRO: It could cost you your life.

CESAR: It could cost you yours. It's the price we have to pay in this game.

NAVARRO: As you wish, then. Listen, there's still time, even for the university deal. We could work something out. Let me go first this time... then you can have your turn. We can run things between the two of us.

CESAR: You're such a stupid fool. I wouldn't be a bit surprised if you tried to kill me. I am surprised you haven't done that already.

NAVARRO: I'm not that much of a fool.

CESAR: Go on, get out.

NAVARRO *(he heads towards the door. Suddenly, he turns around):* Listen, here, I want you to call Salinas back... he's been trying to pick a fight.

CESAR: So, you're afraid to fight face to face. It's only natural. *(Goes to the door. He calls out.)* Salinas! *(NAVARRO smiles to himself.)*

SALINAS *(coming in)*: At your service, General, sir.

CESAR: Stay right here while "General" Navarro is going out. I believe he's a little afraid.

(The sound of a car starting can be heard outside.)

NAVARRO; You've issued your own death sentence "General" Rubio.

SALINAS *(reaching for his gun)*: General?

CESAR *(staying his hand):* Don't waste your bullets. All you have to do is apply some heat and he'll melt away like butter.

(After casting one last look, NAVARRO exits saying:)

NAVARRO: It'll be exactly what you asked for.

(Exits right. A moment later, the sound of cars leaving can be heard.)

SALINAS: General, sir. He's up to no good. I think that we should put a stop to that. Just let me.

CESAR: No, Salinas, let him be. He can't do anything. *(He walks towards center stage and he sees MIGUEL entering from the left door, looking very pale. Steps can be heard on the stairs.)* Miguel! Were you there all along?

MIGUEL *(with a strange voice):* No... I brought you your hat. *(Hands it over.)*

CESAR: What's wrong.

MIGUEL: Nothing.

(At that point ELENA enters from the left and GUZMAN, TREVIÑO and ESTRELLA come in from the right.)

CESAR: It's time to go, boys.

ELENA: Cesar, I need to talk to you for a moment.

CESAR: It'll have to be brief, Elena. That's why I took the time to say goodbye earlier. Boys, go get the cars ready; I'll catch up with you right away. *(MIGUEL, heads towards the left.)* Aren't you coming with us, Miguel?

MIGUEL *(he stops, hesitates, visibly. Finally, making an effort)*: No. *(They all look at him. He realizes he has to offer an explanation.)* I'm not feeling very well *(Quickly.)* If I feel better in a little bit, I'll catch up with you and see you there. *(He avoids speaking directly to his father; he doesn't look at him. Barely managing to finish speaking he hurries out through the left door.)*

CESAR: Let's go, boys. You can go ahead of us.

GUZMAN *(as they leave):* We'll have to have a good escort. I don't trust that Navarro. He was laughing when he got in his car.

(GUZMAN, TREVIÑO and SALINAS exit, talking among themselves.)

ESTRELLA *(he stops at the door, walks back a few steps):* May I ask, General, sir, how was your conversation?

CESAR: It went very well. Don't worry about a thing, Señor Estrella. Go ahead and go. *(ESTRELLA exits.)*

ELENA: What conversation? So, it's true that Navarro was here? That's what I wanted to ask you.

CESAR: Yes, he came by.

ELENA: What did he want?

CESAR: To win, of course. But he lost.

ELENA: Cesar, don't go to the polls.

CESAR *(laughing)*: You remind me of Caesar's wife... the Roman. *(Goes over to her and holds her hands.)* Are you afraid?

ELENA: Yes, I am. Why don't you give everything up, Cesar? You know that Navarro can...

CESAR: Navarro can't do anything anymore. He's finished. While he was here he lost his fangs and his claws.

ELENA: He can still kill you.

CESAR: He's not that kind of fool.

ELENA: Why would you want to risk your life for a lie? Don't do it, Cesar, let's go away and live in peace.

CESAR: I told you: everything together with you, remember? You're talking about a lie. What lie?

ELENA: Don't you know?

CESAR: The fact is, Elena, there's no lie anymore. It was a necessary thing at first in order that the truth may come out. But now I have become real, don't you understand? Now I feel as if I were the other Cesar... I'll do everything he could have accomplished, and more. I'll win the election... I'll become the governor, maybe the President, who knows...

ELENA: But you won't be yourself.

CESAR: You mean to say that you still don't believe in me? But I'll be myself, more than ever. Only the others will think that I am someone else. I had always wondered why destiny had left me out of its game, why it had not put me to good use. It was like not being alive. But now it's different and I can't complain. I am living out the dream I always had. Sometimes I have to look at myself in the mirror to believe it.

ELENA: It isn't destiny, Cesar, but you and your ambitions. Why do you have to have power?

CESAR: You'd be surprised to know. I'll do a lot less harm than others, perhaps I'll even do some good. It is my opportunity and I must take advantage of it. Julia will feel more attractive... I can already see a change in her, when she looks at me; she'll have more suitors than she can handle. Miguel will be able to succeed and do something truly exceptional, if he wants to. And you... *(He embraces her.)* it will be as if you married again, a completely new man... you'll be able to choose the life you want. Finally, you'll have anything you want.

ELENA: I don't want anything. Please don't go to the polls, I beg you.

CESAR: Only death would keep me from going. Now the die is cast, there's no turning around. I have no choice but to go on, Elena; I am the axle in the wheel. But I feel as if the dead man is not Cesar

Rubio but the person I used to be... do you understand? All that dead weight, that inactivity, all that failure that I used to drag around. Tell me you understand and that you will be waiting for me. *(He hugs her, kisses her and puts his hat on.)*

ELENA: Cesar, for the last time, don't go!

CESAR: What are you afraid of?

ELENA: I won't tell you. It might bring you bad luck.

CESAR *(smiling)*: I'll be back soon, Elena. When I return you'll be the governor's wife. *(Looks at her for a moment, then he leaves. Outside a cheering crowd awaits him. ELENA remains in the same place, looking toward the door. Suddenly CESAR reappears.)* You'd better talk to Miguel. I am a bit concerned about him; he was acting very strangely a short while ago. I think he knows something. Elena, why don't you please reassure him? *(He waves a final good bye and exits.)*

(Now alone, ELENA walks up to the poster. She looks at it for a moment, lost in thought. MIGUEL can be heard coming down the stairs. ELENA turns around.)

MIGUEL: Mother, I need to talk to you.

ELENA: Son, I am terribly concerned about your father. I'll be counting the minutes until he comes back.

MIGUEL: If he wins, when he comes back I'll be counting the minutes until I get out of here.

ELENA: Why do you say that?

MIGUEL *(bluntly)*: Why did Father have to do that?

ELENA *(sitting down on the sofa)*: Do what?

MIGUEL: That lie... that fraud.

ELENA: What are you talking about?

MIGUEL: I know he's not Cesar Rubio. Why did he have to lie?

ELENA: I could tell you that he didn't lie.

MIGUEL: I'm sure you could. So what. I wouldn't believe you after what I heard.

ELENA: What is it that you heard, Miguel?

MIGUEL: The truth. I heard it from Navarro.

ELENA: He's one of your father's enemies! How could you believe him?

MIGUEL: I also heard it from another of my father's enemies... his worst enemy. Himself.

ELENA: When?

MIGUEL: A short while ago, when he was arguing with Navarro. You too, go ahead and become a liar, if you want to.

ELENA: Miguel!

MIGUEL: How am I supposed to judge my father... and you... after all this?

ELENA *(reacting firmly):* Judge us? Since when can children judge their parents?

MIGUEL: I want, I need to know why he did this. I will not rest until I find out.

ELENA: When you were born your father told me, 'My son will be all I could never be and do all I could never do. He will overcome my shortcomings and be redemption for all that has failed me.'

MIGUEL: That is the past. You don't expect me to believe that he lied on my behalf, to help me become somebody.

ELENA: It's the present, Miguel. Take a good look at yourself and be your own judge, see if you have lived up to his expectations.

MIGUEL: Has he lived up to mine? Right after we came here I asked him not to do anything dishonest or dirty. I had every right to ask him, and he promised.

ELENA: He has done nothing dishonest or dirty.

MIGUEL: You don't think it's bad enough? To steal someone else's identity and to use it to satisfy his own personal ambition.

ELENA: It was but a moment ago he was expressing concern for you; he thought that his victory might help you fulfill your own dreams. Is this how you repay him?

MIGUEL: What I don't want is his victory... he has no right to win using someone else's name.

ELENA: He has waited all his life to do something important... not only for himself but for me and for you and Julia.

MIGUEL: Is that why you justify him, then? Because he will shower you with money and possessions?

ELENA: You really don't know your mother, Miguel. Your father is not hurting anyone. The other man is dead and there is a lot of good that your father can do in this name. Your father is an honest man.

MIGUEL: No, he is not! He is dishonest and that's what hurts me the most. Had he remained poor I would have helped him, I would have done anything for him. But this way... I don't ever want to see him again.

ELENA *(with dismay)*: That's hatred, Miguel.

MIGUEL: What else did you expect?

ELENA: You can't hate your own father.

MIGUEL: I have tried not to… at first because of the stagnant mediocrity and the stifling falsehood of our lives. All my childhood wasted living by appearances, pretending to be something we were not. Later, at the university, as I watched him defend the system and all those lies.

ELENA: Miguel! Are you forgetting that you… ?

MIGUEL: No. But now this. It's just too much. No wonder I felt anxious, uncomfortable, and ashamed every time I heard the cheers, the applause, the speeches. He has managed to perfect the art of lying that I so much despise, and that is what he did for me, for his son. I will never be able to hear Cesar Rubio's name without dying of shame.

ELENA *(she stands up, flustered):* I couldn't begin to tell you how much you hurt me, Miguel. There must be something wrong with you to make you think and say things like that.

MIGUEL: Why did my own father have to do something like this?

ELENA: Didn't you just say that it was blind ambition, that your own mother had something to do with it? Didn't you just say that nothing would make you change your mind? What's the point of talking to you because you wouldn't understand. I don't recognize you, that's all there's to it… I can't believe that it was you I carried inside of me as a child.

MIGUEL: Mother, don't you understand?

ELENA: All I can understand is that it felt as if I was still carrying you within me, that you were still in my womb and suddenly you had started tearing yourself away.

MIGUEL: Don't you realize that I need the truth to be able to live; that I hunger and crave for the truth, that I feel suffocated in this atmosphere of lies?

ELENA: There's something wrong with you.

MIGUEL: It's a terrible disease, don't think I don't know it. But you can cure me... you can explain to me...

ELENA *(looking at him with compassion):* Sit down, Miguel. *(She sits down on the couch; he sits down at her feet).*

MIGUEL *(as he sits down):* What can you tell me that would erase what I heard from my own father?

ELENA: I can tell you that he did not lie.

MIGUEL *(raising his head violently):* If you are lying, too, Mother, that will be the end of everything for me.

ELENA *(forcefully):* Your father did not lie. He never said to anyone: I am General Cesar Rubio. To no one... not even to Bolton. He believed it, and your father let him; he gave legitimate documents to Bolton in exchange for money so that he could give all of us a better life.

MIGUEL: But he had promised me... I can't believe it.

ELENA: Weren't you right there that afternoon when all those politicians came to see him? Did you hear him say once that he was General Cesar Rubio? *(MIGUEL shakes his head without saying anything.)* Then why are you accusing him? Why did you say all those terrible things?

MIGUEL *(passionately, again):* Why did he go along with this whole farce, then? Why didn't he put a stop to it? Granted, he did not say: I am General Rubio, but he did not say that he wasn't either. And it was so easy! All it took was one word, but instead, he has been carried away by all this... he has fooled himself into thinking that he is a general or some kind of hero. It's ridiculous. How could it be? If I had a son I would feed him nothing but the truth, I would feed him the truth like milk, like air.

ELENA: If you had a son, you would give him nothing but grief. I've told you why your father decided to go along with it. He'll be a good leader, this is his chance, what he has always dreamed about; he'll be able to give his children what they never had before. What would you do in his place, if your children had always considered you a failure and, if you were offered the opportunity to do something... important?

MIGUEL: There's nothing more important than the truth. My father will govern in place of those thieves... he said that himself; but those thieves at least are themselves, not the ghost of a dead man.

ELENA: He didn't even take his name... that was his name, they were born in the same town...

MIGUEL: No... no... not this way, not like this. I would rather have him, any time, as he used to be when he was at the university.

ELENA: You're too young, Miguel. Your judgement, your ideas, are violent and harsh. You hurl them like stones and they crumble like dust. Before at the university you used to accuse your father of being a failure; now...

MIGUEL: That was a lot better. A lot better than this. Now I can see.

(JULIA enters from the left. Clearly, she has been listening to part of this conversation. MIGUEL stands up and walks toward the window.)

JULIA: What is it, Mother?

ELENA: Nothing.

JULIA: I know there's something wrong.

MIGUEL *(turning around, still by the window)*: You've been listening, haven't you. Hiding on the stairs...

JULIA: Exactly the same way you heard what you were not supposed to; the conversation between Father and Navarro. I saw you from upstairs. Why didn't you have the guts to tell father these things directly, face to face?

ELENA: Julia!

JULIA: For me, no matter what happens, Father will always be a great man… a hero. If you'd only watched him these past few days, giving orders, talking to the people, bringing the political bosses to heel, you would have seen that he was born to be a leader. He had to wait for a long time, but he deserved to have this opportunity to…

MIGUEL: You are a woman. I'm not surprised that your worst instincts were awakened by hero worship. That's what seduced you. If I didn't watch him it is because I was watching you. Anyone who didn't know you were his daughter would have thought you were in love with him. And besides, of course, his heroism will bring you what you've always wanted: clothes, jewelry, cars.

ELENA: Miguel, I forbid you!

JULIA: All I can hear coming out of your mouth is your inferiority complex, your envy…

MIGUEL: But I'm no liar!

JULIA: He was a good teacher; you were a poor student. Now, deep down, you wish you were in his place, you wish you were the hero. But you don't have what it takes.

MIGUEL: You fool! You can't recognize the truth even if it's staring you in the face. How could you… you are a woman. You need to have lies to be able to live. You are as stupid as if all you had was a pretty face.

ELENA *(standing between them):* That's enough, Miguel!

JULIA: You're not really hurting me with that. What is my plain face compared to your cowardice? Because your obsession with the truth is nothing but the sickly passion of a coward. A person carries the truth within, not on the surface.

ELENA: Julia!

MIGUEL: Believe that if you want. I'll go on searching for the truth.

(Pause, JULIA walks up to the table, picks up the telegrams and reads them one by one, with satisfaction. ELENA sits down. MIGUEL fixed to the window, looks out.)

JULIA: Look Mother, this one is from the President. *(Carries it over to her.)*

ELENA *(she receives the telegram, but doesn't look at it):* Miguel…

MIGUEL: Yes, Mother?

ELENA: Did you hear everything your father and Navarro talked about?

MIGUEL: Almost everything.

ELENA: Then, you need to tell me…

MIGUEL: I don't remember anything… what I heard filled my ears so that I couldn't hear anymore.

ELENA: Did Navarro threaten your father?

MIGUEL: I suppose so.

ELENA: Try to remember… it's very important. He makes me terribly anxious. What did he say? How did he threaten your father?

MIGUEL: Why is it so important? Father can't lose the election, can he?

ELENA: Miguel! Please, think hard, do it for me.

MIGUEL *(after a pause):* Now I remember. When he said goodbye Navarro told him: "You've issued your own death sentence… It'll be exactly what you asked for."

ELENA *(standing up):* Miguel, your father is in danger, and you knew it all along and here you are saying all those things about him…

MIGUEL *(taking one step forward):* Couldn't you tell how I felt… how I feel now?

ELENA: But your father is in danger!

MIGUEL: Didn't he ask for it? Didn't he lie?

ELENA: You must go, Miguel. You must protect him.

(MIGUEL hesitates.)

JULIA: He's afraid, Mother, that's all there's to it. I'll go.

ELENA: I knew it. I knew it. *(She wrings her hands.)* Navarro is going to try to kill him. *(JULIA runs to the door, at the same time that...)*

MIGUEL *(reacting abruptly):* You're right, Mother. I'm sorry about everything, please forgive me. I'll go... I'll try to protect him, but afterwards... It'll be between him and me, face to face. *(Leaves running.)*

JULIA: Nothing will happen, Mother, I have all the confidence in him now!

ELENA: I don't know... I don't know. Deep down, Miguel...

JULIA: Miguel is crazy, Mother... he searches for the truth like a fanatic, as if the truth wasn't possible. Don't pay attention to him.

ELENA: He's in such a state now... and you, too. The things you two said to each other...

JULIA *(with a smile)*: We've always done that, Mother, ever since we were children. That's the way Miguel worked up his courage to fight, to show me that he was not a coward.

ELENA: You were very hard...

JULIA: But I wouldn't let anyone else talk to him like that.

ELENA: I don't know... I really don't know. *(As if somewhat hypnotized by her anxiety.)* What time is it?

JULIA: It's noon, Mother. Look at the sun. Now I can tell the time by looking at the sun. *(ELENA, somewhat dazed, walks up to the window. There she stretches both arms so as to touch both sides; with her head tilted backwards she stares intensely outside. JULIA continues reading telegrams underscoring her interest with small gestures of satisfaction. ELENA looks like a statue. JULIA looks at her.)*

JULIA: Calm down, Mother, please. He will be back in a short while and everything will change for us... even Miguel.

ELENA *(without turning around):* I can't. A moment ago I felt the sun like a heavy blow on my chest.

JULIA: Do it for him. He wouldn't like to see you like this.

ELENA: Miguel is right. Nothing good can come out of a lie. Yet, I couldn't find the way to stop Cesar.

JULIA: There's no lie, Mother. Everything in the past was a dream, this is real. I don't care about the clothes and the jewelry, as Miguel believes. I care about the new air we breathe. The air that comes from father's power. From now on it will be like living in the highest building in this town; later, in the tallest one in all of Mexico. You haven't heard him give speeches at meetings; you have no idea how much he can give, someone who was so poor. You can't even imagine how much he has to offer.

ELENA: I don't want anything, Julia. I just want him to live. And I'm scared.

JULIA: I'm not. For me, he's like the light. Everybody can see him, nobody can touch him. It will be wonderful, Mother, to be able to do everything, to think thoughts with wings; not like before, when all my wishes, my dreams felt like reptiles trapped within me.

ELENA *(sits down):* Maybe you are thinking about your boyfriend, and that's why you are talking like that. Do you really expect that boy to continue to have an interest in you after he sees that you are so unreachable? I wouldn't approve of him, then: it would be for the wrong reasons.

JULIA: I don't love him anymore, Mother. I've known that for two weeks now. What I loved in him was what I lacked around me and in me. But now I have it and he doesn't matter to me. I will have to look in another man for the things I don't have. Every woman seeks to do better.

ELENA: I'm afraid, Julia. These past weeks, while Cesar was traveling around the state, I thought at night about the man he has yet to become, the man I have to learn to love. If Cesar is chosen...

JULIA: He has already been chosen, Mother. He's the chosen one.

ELENA: If they choose Cesar, he'll become the Governor. He'll be surrounded by people every moment of the day, people who will help him get dressed, who will keep him away from me. He will own so many clothes that he will not like any in particular... and I won't have to sew any of them, I won't have to iron his shirts or take stains out of his suit. One way or another, it will seem as if they took him away from me. And I don't want him to go away. *(She stands up abruptly.)* He must lose that election, Julia, he must.

JULIA: Have you lost your mind? Don't you understand what all this means to all of us? Haven't you ever wished that the light would shine on you? It will be a new life for all of us.

ELENA: You sound like your father.

JULIA: I will lay out his clothes every morning in such a way that he will not be able to touch his tie or feel his suit over his body without touching me or sensing me. With you he will discuss his ideas, his plans, all his decisions, and when he carries them out he will be seeing you and feeling your presence.

ELENA: He didn't listen to me... he doesn't want to listen to me. But why? Why? No. I don't care if he loses or they find out about him, I don't care if everybody make fun of him and of his lie. Miguel was right. I don't care if they curse his name or spit on him...

JULIA: Don't talk like that! Why are you talking like that?

ELENA: I'll comfort him. But I want him to live.

JULIA: You want him to die.

ELENA: I want the ghost to die, I want him to live; I want him to die a natural death, his own death. I want him alive. *(Pause. In the quiet of the midday hour the sound of a car horn can be heard very close by. ELENA is startled.)* A car!

JULIA *(running to the window, speaking)*: Mother, it's Guzmán and Miguel.

ELENA: Can you see other cars?

(JULIA does not reply. ELENA stays motionless, center stage, looking at the door. JULIA moves next to her. MIGUEL and GUZMAN come in.)

ELENA: Miguel… *(Long pause. MIGUEL lowers his head without saying a word.)*

JULIA: What happened?

GUZMAN *(breathing heavily)*: Señora…

ELENA: Was Cesar hurt? *(GUZMAN lowers his head.)* No… he's dead, isn't he?

GUZMAN: I found the boy along the road, Señora, he was running. It was too late.

ELENA *(composed)*: What happened? Was it Navarro?

GUZMAN: As far as I am concerned, Señora, it was him. But they killed the assassin right then and there. One shot, that's all it took. We had just arrived and the General was about to sit down when… Right in his heart.

JULIA: Mother…

(She grabs her hands. Their pain is beyond words, an excruciating pain that unfolds and restrains itself ever so slowly.)

ELENA: Did you say that they killed the man who fired the shot?

GUZMAN: The people tore him to pieces, Señora. *(The noise of car motors can be heard outside.)*

ELENA *(slowly, in a low voice):* Pieces.

(She turns around facing the wall, standing very erect. JULIA weeps quietly, barely lowering her head, her tears rolling down. MIGUEL drops down into a chair. Voices can be heard now. NAVARRO appears at the entrance.)

GUZMAN: You! How dare you!

NAVARRO: Señora, allow me to express my most sincere condolences to you. Your husband was the victim of a most cowardly murder.

(MIGUEL walks behind them and closes the door.)

GUZMAN: Cowardly is the right word. I also have a good idea who is the murderer.

MIGUEL *(front, right):* So do I.

NAVARRO *(unperturbed):* Cesar Rubio's assassin, Señora was a Catholic fanatic.

GUZMAN: It was you!

NAVARRO: It was most certainly a fanatic. A cross and some scapulars were found on his body.

GUZMAN: What's the point of blaming someone else? We know perfectly well who…

ELENA *(livid):* I think you should leave now, General Navarro. How dare you come here after… *(She is interrupted by a growing com-*

motion outside which becomes a rising storm of voices. NAVARRO bows, walks towards the door, and opens it, casting a glance at the family as he exits. Angry grumbling can be heard. Then, more and more distinctly NAVARRO's voice speaking loud.)

NAVARRO'S VOICE: My friends! I have come here today to express to Cesar Rubio's widow my profound indignation over the heinous murder of her husband. Although there is sufficient proof that the murder was committed by a Catholic fanatic, there are those who dare accuse me. *(Hostile murmur. GUZMAN walks to the door and exits.)* I am prepared to defend myself in a court of law and to renounce my candidacy until I am proven innocent...

GUZMAN"S VOICE: That's a lie! He's lying! He's the murderer and everybody knows it!

(Hostile murmur but declining in intensity.)

NAVARRO'S VOICE: I will not dignify that with a comment. Cesar Rubio was killed by reactionary forces while defending our revolutionary ideals. I felt great admiration for him. I went to the polls prepared to withdraw my candidacy in his favor because I felt he was the kind of leader we all needed. *(Expressions of approval.)* But, if I am elected, I will make the memory of Cesar Rubio, a martyr of the Revolution who fell victim to a fanatic, reactionary conspiracy, into the most cherished of all. I always admired him as a great leader. The state capital will bear his name, we will build a university in his memory, a true monument to remind future generations... *(He is interrupted by a clamor of approval.)* And the widow and the children of Cesar Rubio will be treated as if he were the Governor. *(Muffled applause.)*

ELENA *(waving a hand that seems broken):* Shut it, Miguel. The doors, the windows; shut everything.

MIGUEL: No, Mother. The entire world must know, they will know... I couldn't go on living like the son of a ghost.

ELENA *(shattered):* Shut it, Julia. It's all over now.

(JULIA, defeated now, walks up to the window and shuts it first, then, the door. Semi-darkness. The noise from outside becomes less audible.)

MIGUEL: Mother! *(He sobs quietly.)*

ELENA: That's someone else. Our Cesar… *(She cannot go on. A knock at the door.)* Don't answer, Julia.

(More knocking at the door. MIGUEL opens the door slowly. ESTRELLA comes in followed by SALINAS and GUZMAN.)

ESTRELLA *(with the self-satisfied, pompous solemnity of a third-rate politician):* Señora, the President has been duly informed of this most grievous incident *(MIGUEL listens facing them.)* The body of General Rubio will lay in state at the Governor's palace. I've come to escort all of you there. He will receive the honors due a governor; but, in addition, and taking into consideration the fact that he was a five-star general and a great hero, he will be accorded presidential honors and his body will lay in state in the national Rotunda of Illustrious Men. You, Señora, will receive the benefits of a governor's pension. The revolutionary government will not forget the family of its greatest hero.

ELENA: Thank you, but I don't want any of that. I just want to have the body of my husband. I will go claim it. *(Walks toward the door. JULIA follows her.)* You stay here.

JULIA: We'll all go, Mother. And he will receive full honors. *(ELENA looks at her.)* Don't you see… ?

SALINAS: I don't understand, Señora.

ESTRELLA: Cesar Rubio belongs to the people, Señora.

GUZMAN *(speaking from behind, angrily):* He belongs to us forever.

JULIA: Don't you see, Mother? He will be my beauty.

(ELENA makes an effort to speak, but unsuccessfully. Makes a feeble attempt at raising her hand. ESTRELLA holds her by the arm. They

exit. MIGUEL remains alone on the stage. The voices and sounds from the crowd outside come to a respectful hush upon seeing the widow. A moment later NAVARRO comes in.)

MIGUEL: You? There's something I have to clear up, first, with you, then with the rest.

NAVARRO *(brutally)*: So, what is it that you know?

MIGUEL: I know that you killed my father. *(With unrestrained force.)* I know it. I heard your conversation!

NAVARRO *(taken aback)*: Yes? *(Regaining his composure.)* Young man, listen to what the people are saying, and they watched the incident. The man who fired the shot was a Catholic fanatic. I have proof. My own men tried to catch him.

MIGUEL: And just to make sure, they killed him to destroy all proof. You had my father murdered and then you killed the man who fired the shot, the same way you killed Cesar Rubio. I heard everything!

NAVARRO *(confused and embarrassed)*: Your grief doesn't let you... *(Suddenly defiant.)* You can't prove anything!

MIGUEL: I can't do anything about that. But I am not going to let you go on with this farce: The state capital named after him, the university, the pension benefits. You know very well that my father was not Cesar Rubio!

NAVARRO: Have you gone crazy? Your father <u>was</u> Cesar Rubio. How can you go against the belief of an entire people? I couldn't.

MIGUEL: You killed him. Was that easier?

NAVARRO: Your father was a hero who deserves to be remembered and whose memory must be respected.

MIGUEL: I cannot allow such a grotesque lie to continue. I will put a stop to it and tell the truth right now.

NAVARRO: When you calm down, young man, you'll be able to understand where your real duty lies. I'm able to understand it, even though your father was my political opponent. Any man who sheds his blood for his country is a hero. And Mexico needs her heroes to survive. Your father was a martyr of the Revolution.

MIGUEL: That's sickening! You make Mexico sound like a bloodthirsty vampire... but that's not what matters to me... it's the truth I care about, and I intent to shout it to the four winds.

NAVARRO *(reaches for his gun. MIGUEL stares at him defiantly. NAVARRO thinks it over and smiles.)* Nobody will believe you. If you persist in your ravings I'll have you committed to a mental institution.

MIGUEL *(with cold fury):* Yes, I know you would. But, even if it kills me...

NAVARRO: They'll laugh at you. You can't take away from the people what is theirs. If you say anything in public they'll think you're crazy. *(He gives a mock salute to a poster of Cesar Rubio.)* Your father was a great hero.

MIGUEL: I will find proof that my father was not a hero and you are a murderer.

NAVARRO *(at the door):* What proof? You'll have to prove one thing or the other. If you accuse me of being a murderer, some misguided people might believe you; but since you also maintain that your father was a fraud, then nobody will believe a word of what you say. Young man, you are my best defense and your father was certainly a great man. I owe him the election. *(He exits. An indistinct clamor can be heard outside, then, voices that shout: Viva Navarro!)*

NAVARRO'S VOICE: No, no, boys! Long live Cesar Rubio! *(A thunderous "Viva Cesar Rubio" can be heard.)*

(MIGUEL makes a movement toward the door, then he quickly exits left. Outside sounds of voices and car engines running. A brief pause at the end of which MIGUEL reappears carrying a small suitcase. Goes

to the door on the right. From there he returns, puts the suitcase down and takes down the poster of Cesar Rubio. He folds the poster silently and puts it down on the desk. Then he pushes the roll of posters with his foot; the roll unfolds like a fan showing multiple images of Cesar Rubio.)

MIGUEL: The truth!

(He covers his face with his hand for a moment and seems on the verge of surrender, but he stands up. Then, showing despair he grabs the suitcase. At the door he makes sure that there is nobody outside. The sunlight is blinding. MIGUEL exits, fleeing the very shadow of Cesar Rubio, which will haunt him the rest of his life.)

CURTAIN

(Left) Poster for a 1962 production of *El gesticulador* in Nova Huta, Poland. (Rodolfo Usigli Archive, Miami University Libraries, Oxford, Ohio).

(Bottom) Poster for 1972 production of *El gesticulador* in Bogotá, Colombia by the Teatro Popular de Bogotá. Adapted and directed by Luis Alberto García. (Rodolfo Usigli Archive, Miami University Libraries, Oxford, Ohio).

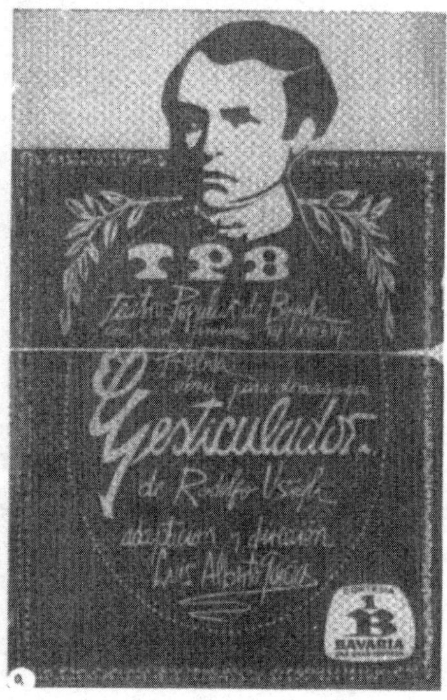